Dirty Faxes

Andrew Davies was born in Cardiff and lives in Warwickshire. His plays, *Prin* and *Rose*, were highly praised in the West End and New York, and he has won numerous awards for his work for television, which includes *A Very Peculiar Practice*, *Mother Love* and *House of Cards*. His first novel, *Getting Hurt*, was published in 1989 to great acclaim, and is also available in Minerva.

Andrew Davies

Dirty Faxes

AND OTHER STORIES

Minerva

A Minerva Paperback
DIRTY FAXES

First published in Great Britain 1990
by Methuen London
This Minerva edition published 1991
Reprinted 1991 (twice)
by Mandarin Paperbacks
Michelin House, 81 Fulham Road, London SW3 6RB

Minerva is an imprint of the Octopus Publishing Group,
a division of Reed International Books Limited

A CIP catalogue record for this title
is available from the British Library
ISBN 0 7493 9903 1

Printed and bound in Great Britain
by Cox & Wyman Ltd, Reading, Berks

CONTENTS

Keeping It Clean

Scannell is finding it hard to concentrate. Everything is as it should be, everything is to hand: the meticulous notes on Eye Contact, Magazine Strategy and Non-Verbal Signs in the Outpatients' Clinic; the computer read-out correlating age, social class, sex and ailment. Outside the window the morning traffic has thinned to a helpful drone; somewhere upstairs the Hoover booms reassuringly; on the desk in front of him the Amstrad glows invitingly. But somehow he can't get started.

Scannell prefers to do his serious work at home, in his own front room. His wife is happily and lucratively at work, his children deposited grumbling at their schools, and his dog Betsy, a mild and silly Alsatian bitch, who prefers the company of the three other members of the family, nevertheless enjoys Scannell's companionship in a resigned sort of way. And lately Scannell has been finding the atmosphere at the Poly increasingly disturbing; gradually his department has been swelling underneath him with younger, thinner men, who practise neo-Marxist objectivity (Scannell privately finds this a contradiction in terms) and outmanoeuvre and outlast him at meetings, clearly regarding him as a spent force, an irrelevant survival of dilettante bourgeois meliorism.

Scannell is thirty-seven years old; the study he is about to begin is crucial to his re-establishment, his Re-Presentation of Self in Academic Life. It is a model of classic Social Psychology, brilliantly meshed into the realities of contemporary social intercourse. It will put him up there with Argyle and Goffman. It may even get him to the States. Why can't he get his finger out?

Scannell is the department's specialist in Body Language, though he has not had much luck with it himself. Hart, the beefy South African Reader in Social Administration, breezes daily through the corridors and cafeterias enacting token mountings on his colleagues, his huge hairy hands pushing them down into the chairs, massaging academic shoulders to the point of dislocation. Hart humiliates and baffles the neo-Marxists simply by bear-hugging them and tousling their hair. He has not published since 1976. Scannell's specialism enables him to understand Hart's success, but he shrinks from emulating his technique. For some time, he has been practising furtive Hart-moves on Betsy, muttering gruff endearments as he shakes her by the scruff and thumps her rump, but it is hard to gauge her response. He suspects that it is one of fear and loathing.

Or take Landon, he thinks. Landon is less exalted in the department than Hart, though he receives the confidences of every member of it including Scannell, and enjoys a sexual and emotional life of truly alarming complexity. This is because Landon (through a combination of short sight and some faulty social skills learning) conducts all his conversations at a face-to-face range of nine or ten inches. More than once, when discussing some mundane matter of timetables or examination marking with Landon, Scannell has felt a strong impulse to lean closer and kiss his colleague. Nothing queer about Scannell, or Landon, as far as he knows: it is simply that statistically ninety-four per cent of nine-inch conversations are followed by acts of physical intimacy. Scannell knows all this, none better; but his few personal explorations into this field have been disastrous enough to drive him to the Listerine bottle and some glum self-searching.

Time is going by and nothing's getting done. He must not let another day drag out in self-contempt and afternoon TV. He must use his analytical powers. He must isolate the source of his anomie and neutralise it. He must ask himself the right question. And suddenly, he has it. It's the Hoover. It is not a reassuring boom at all: it is the insistent reminder of another person in the house, another social unit, another breathing presence. Subconsciously, he has been waiting for Julie to come downstairs and take her coffee break.

Julie is the cleaning lady, and the source of a good deal of category-confusion, social guilt and head-scratching on Scannell's part. Her very title is a source of embarrassment. All very well in the advertisement: 'Domestic Help Wanted.' But domestic help is not what she is, it is what she gives. Cleaning Lady sounds so genteel and pissy. And though Scannell's wife and all her female friends are (of course) Women, Julie is not, cannot be, a Cleaning Woman. One might as well call her the nigger and have done with it. Cleaning Person? Sounds so impersonal. Cleaner? Ah, but she is more than that. When he has to refer to her, Scannell resorts to circumlocutions – this woman who comes in on Wednesdays to help out, sort of thing – or simply says Julie, which causes confusion in his colleagues of a kind obscurely pleasing to Scannell. But it is not satisfactory. He would like to know how to refer to her in his private thoughts. Is she the cleaning lady, or is she Julie? Craske and the rest of the neo-Marxists would say that his difficulty is nothing to do with nice social distinctions: it results from the relationship, which is one of straightforward capitalist exploitation. Scannell takes the point. But there is more to it than this, much more; problems of such richness and complexity that Scannell doubts if Social Psychology has yet devised an analytical instrument of sufficient subtlety to tease them out.

Things were so much simpler in the days of Mrs Eggins. Mrs Eggins was a Cleaning Lady with no category-confusion at all. Six feet tall in her Scholls, thirteen stone and most of it muscle, she was a demon of domestic help, an enthusiast who destroyed Hoover parts not through clumsiness but through the sheer exuberance and force of her movements. She scrubbed the pattern off the Cushionflor, hoovered the shagpile into alopecia, the very walls seemed thinner when she had gone home. She called Scannell Mr Scannell and no mucking about, and he called her Mrs Eggins. She needed nothing from him but Vim, polish and a little money, and she treated him with jovial contempt.

Scannell sighs loudly and lays his cheek against the cool flank of the Amstrad. At least – he suddenly thinks – at least I didn't fancy her. I didn't even like her. Scannell isn't used to insights. He is a slow, deductive reasoner. Even now he doesn't make the connection that you and I have leapt to instantly – Scannell's trouble with Julie is that he both likes and fancies her. Give him a little while. He'll get to it.

Half past ten and not a word written. Scannell despises himself. Just one sentence, he tells himself, just one little trickle of type to start the flow, unlock the flood . . . and above him, the Hoover's roar changes to a desolate descending moan and shudders into silence. Scannell is at once alert; back straight, heart thumping, ears straining for the soft footsteps down the stairs, the pause as she stands on the other side of the door . . . go on!

There is a tap at the door and before he can speak it has opened and she stands there.

'Like a cup of coffee, Alan?' She speaks his name with timid bravery, making it sound more personal than it usually does.

'Good idea. Thanks a lot.' Scannell marvels at the even, casual tone he has achieved. Attempting a jaunty whistle, he follows her into the kitchen.

She plugs the kettle in, turns and leans against the fridge, and Scannell registers, not for the first time, the slightness and paleness of her body. (His wife, who also leans on fridges, is tall and muscular.) Julie's cheeks are flushed from Hoovering the stairs and she is breathing audibly. Her parted lips glisten with saliva. Scannell can see her tongue! Her hair – wavy, dark gold with an undertow of red – is tousled, and one damp strand clings to her forehead. All this reminds Scannell of something, but he can't for the moment think what.

'Warmer today,' she says.

'Yes.' His voice sounds hoarse. Pull yourself together, Scannell. 'How are you then, Julie?'

'Oh,' she sighs. 'Not so bad. Tony's gone back on nights again. I don't sleep well when he's on nights. Keep waking up and, you know, panicking . . . then I remember.'

Scannell has a sudden, unbidden image of her tossing restlessly in a big empty bed, a strand of hair stuck to her forehead . . . What's the matter with him?

'Snoring in his pit now, is he?'

'Oh, yes,' she sighs. 'He can get off anywhere, any time. He's lucky like that.'

A plume of steam rises between them and she turns and makes the coffee. Scannell watches. He wants to be there, but he can't think of anything else to say. She puts two sugars in his, none in hers (sweet enough without it, she told him her first week, causing him some disquiet) and hands him the mug.

'Marvellous!' he says, much too enthusiastically.

'It's only a cup of coffee, Alan.' Her face is childishly serious, then she grins. What does she mean?

'Have you . . . ?' he begins, and then stops, for she has put her mug down and is crouching at his feet! He lets out an involuntary gasp and then turns it into a cough as he sees that she is only rubbing a mark on the washing machine. Nevertheless – his whirling brain tries to reason – this crouching behaviour surely has some significance. He wishes he had noted the number of times she has crouched or knelt in his presence – surely enough for a little article – and then stops thinking altogether as he sees that several buttons of her blouse have come undone. Her bra is old, overwashed, inelastic, and droops away from her little breast. Scannell moves his head two inches and is rewarded by the sight of her left nipple; the palest pink, delicate and unused-looking, as if she were a schoolgirl.

She glances up at him. Is he going mad, or does he read humble compliance in her eyes? For a wild moment he contemplates unzipping, touching her soft head and drawing her flushed lips gently towards his yearning member – then he remembers Landon, Listerine, a lifetime of blunders. There is a lump in his throat. He realises that he is blushing furiously.

'Well!' he manages. 'Got to get on!' Grabs his mug and flees to his Amstrad and an agonised reappraisal of his situation.

The week does not go well for Scannell. Serious work on the

study is out of the question. His new course proposal is voted down at Faculty Board after Craske and his gang have picked away at its liberal evasions and bourgeois category-confusions. Scannell hardly registers the humiliation of defeat. He is deep in his own category-confusion: he is in love with his cleaning lady. And this, he knows very well, is an absurdity. Academic social scientists may conduct extra-marital affairs with colleagues, and the wives (though not the mistresses) of colleagues; they may slake their lust freely on students, except their own students, for whose moral welfare they have professional responsibility. Coming a little nearer to Scannell's own situation, *au pairs* have a long, well-established and respectable tradition as persons into whom it is OK, even *de rigueur*, to dip the seigneurial wick. But cleaning ladies. Cleaning women. Deeply suspect to have to admit to employing one, but to look lewdly upon, to have a bit on the side with, to, oh God, fall in love with . . . !

It is Wednesday again. The Amstrad glows, the Hoover booms, and Scannell moans softly to himself. Today she let herself in without calling a greeting, ran upstairs – Scannell thinks he heard a sniffle or a snuffle, perhaps he could lend her a handkerchief, wipe the bogeys from her tender nostrils, and . . . stop it STOP IT helpless clown – and boomed away at the Hoovering without a pause. It is twenty-five to eleven and he can't stand it a moment longer. He opens the door and goes out into the hall.

'Julie!'

Nothing.

'Julie!' The long despairing howl of the Hoover dies away. 'I'm making some coffee!'

'OK, I'll be down in a minute, Alan.' Her voice sounds flat and resigned, none of that teasing lilt that he detected when she spoke to him a week ago. He has imagined it all. What a prat he is. What a . . . poltroon. Trembling slightly he walks into the kitchen and plugs the kettle in. His ears are buzzing and he feels faintly sick. When she comes in, he thinks, he will not be able to speak a single word.

He has made the coffee and absentmindedly gulped half of his own before she appears in the doorway. There is something different about her face. All week he's been picturing it and now it looks wrong: surely it's thinner. Her eyes look puffy. Her mouth droops. Perhaps he doesn't love her after all. She comes over and takes her mug.

'Thanks, Alan,' she says. Her voice is soft and glum. 'I was meaning to do it but . . .'

She sniffs loudly.

'Sorry.'

Scannell's panic subsides as he sees the tears on her cheeks.

'What's the matter, Julie?'

'Nothing.' She shakes her head and looks away.

He waits.

'It's Tony. You know I said he's started working extra shifts. Well he hasn't been. He's been seeing this woman. I know who she is. It's been going on and off since we were all at school. He says it's all over now, but I don't believe him.'

'Which school?' asks Scannell stupidly.

'Highfields. You know, down the road.' Just down the road, he thinks, put her in uniform and she could still be there. He feels a rush of tenderness, and moving with an ease he has rarely, if ever, achieved before, he takes three steps towards her. Her tear-stained face is nine or ten inches from his.

He touches her shoulder gently. She stares at him for a moment, then with a curious almost angry burrowing movement she pushes her head into his chest and begins to sob noisily. Scannell finds that he has his arms around her small body and all the week's tension, lust and anxiety drain out of him. Everything in the room looks bright and clear: the Habitat jars, the familiar shelf of Elizabeth Davids seem charged with wonder as he holds and comforts his little friend, letting the sobs subside as she trembles against him. He feels something so unfamiliar that he can hardly recognise it. He feels content.

After several mindless minutes he feels something else too, something else besides the content and trembling. More and more perceptibly she is moving her belly against him. The word squirming suggests itself to Scannell, and he rejects it indignantly, but there it stays. Julie is squirming slowly and rhythmically against him, bracing herself against the fridge for better purchase, burying her head deeper and deeper into his chest. This is impossible, thinks Scannell. But a social psychologist's penis is less complicated than his reasoning apparatus, and Scannell's rises confidently to the summons. The movements going on down there become immediately more specific and purposeful, and Scannell, catching his breath, slips his hand into the grubby white blouse.

'Oh, Alan,' she mutters, and at last seems able to raise her head and look at him.

'Look,' he says. 'You don't . . .'

Calmly she takes his free hand in her own and leads him upstairs to the master bedroom.

Scannell has always worried about how, in such circumstances, the business of undressing would be managed. But Julie's clothes seem very sketchily attached to her; and her practice in rushing small children in and out of their clothes enables her to make short work of Scannell. It seems only a few seconds before he is crouching in his socks over her pale downy body, moved almost to tears by the frailness of her, drawn to the paler reddish gold of her pubic hair. Uncharacteristically, he thinks of ferns, fronds, forests, and buries his face in her.

'No,' she sighs. 'No, you mustn't,' her fingers fluttering in his hair, drawing him deeper in. Cunnilingus, for Scannell, has always been more of an arduous duty than a pleasure, to be undertaken conscientiously in a spirit of *quid pro quo* (his wife being a stickler for fair deals) and always faintly unsatisfactory in a gritty, Shredded Wheat sort of way. But now, his nose sunk deep in unfamiliar scents and textures, he's like a pig in clover. He surprises himself. He excels himself. He actually enjoys himself; and his cleaning lady comes quickly in a series of trembling shudders, her thighs closing snugly over his ears and drowning him in silence and darkness.

He barely has time to register the thought that this is all very well, when she has taken him by the ears (by the ears!) and drawn him up over her. How strange her face looks on his blue-and-white Next Interiors pillowslip, her eyes huge and green, her eyelashes almost orange. For a panicky moment he sees her as an entirely new person, a blurred, brightly coloured greedy stranger, then he slips into her (sometimes, even for Scannell, it is that easy) amazed at how much room there is for him in her small body. 'Oh, Alan,' she says, and he stops thinking about anything at all for several minutes.

BUT Scannell can't stop thinking for long. Even at the moment of his last deep thrust, even as he hears his voice crying out, the dark thought sweeps across his brain like a J-cloth over wet Formica, that this is all going to prove a terrible mistake, that he has finally done for himself. Some phrase he has heard somewhere – couldn't be Durkheim, could it? – about the expense of spirit in a waste of shame, or something, is ringing obscurely in his ears.

'Well,' says Julie, moments or hours later, 'that's paid him out, anyway.' It takes Scannell a second or two to realise that she is talking about her husband. He feels affronted, and then faintly comforted. She is helping him to categorise the event.

'You're funny,' she says. 'You're not a bit like I thought you'd be.'

'How d'you mean?'

'Not saying.'

She kisses his cheek and pulls his head down. 'That's better,' she says, and soon he is asleep.

He wakes in a panic to hear Betsy whining at the door.

'Hey,' says Julie. 'I'd better get on.'

'It's not twelve yet, is it?'

'No, but I haven't done half the house yet.'

'Oh, look,' says Scannell. 'You mustn't. Not . . . I mean it doesn't seem . . .'

'Well, what'd Rosemary think? She'd wonder, wouldn't she?'

'I'll help you,' says Scannell.

Seven days pass in fear, confusion, doubt. But Rosemary seems to notice nothing. He has been lucky. Gradually he gets a grip on himself. Next Wednesday he will have a sensible talk with Julie. Wonderful memory, deeply grateful, sensible grown-up people, responsibilities to others, can't let it happen again: all that. If she comes. He wouldn't be surprised if she doesn't. Perhaps it might be all for the best. Oh, Julie!

On Wednesday she lets herself in, booms and rattles away with the Hoover for an hour while Scannell trembles in agonies of apprehension at his silent Amstrad, then at half past ten precisely she makes the coffee, grins at him, and leads him upstairs without a word.

It's been going on for two months now. In those two months Scannell has not written a single word of his study. He has lost interest in it. He would like to write a thesis on sex, class and domestic help, but he knows his wife would read it and guess the truth. She has become more demanding of late, her desires seeming to peak, by cruel coincidence, on Wednesday night. Scannell, never a sexual Stakhanovite, is worn to a frazzle.

And Julie, too, is changing; her demeanour in bed and out of it is more challenging, assertive, even (he fears) critical. After they have made love she is apt to luxuriate in his bed for an hour or more, singing softly to herself and playing with her nipples, while Scannell bangs frantically about the house with Hoover and J-cloth, doing the work he has paid her to do. He often howls aloud under the covering boom of the Hoover, because he has no one to blame but himself. Soon his position in the department will come under review. On his salary scale there is something called an efficiency bar. He does not see how his efficiency with Harpic and lavatory brush could be called up for the defence.

Let's leave him there, shall we, scrubbing steadily at a small, persistent brown stain just below the rim of the lavatory pan, his cleaning lady's soft tuneful voice humming a cheerful song from the bedroom, his dim gloomy reflection staring up at him from the lavatory pan. If I had been an imaginative writer instead of a social psychologist (it suddenly occurs to him) I could have made up a story about all this, instead of having to live it out in the flesh.

Into Europe

Rust opens one eye. The little leprechaun in walking boots who sits opposite him beams and twinkles, and Rust closes his eye again and feigns sleep. Rust feels terrible. His head aches, his back is stiff, he feels nauseous and faint, his athlete's foot is making a comeback, and his heart is broken. He has been up all night on a boat. He should be tucked up safely and snoring in his pit, snug as a bug in a rug, Oblivion County, not dozing fitfully upright in an early morning train out of the Hook of Holland and bound for fuck knows where . . . what was it . . . Wurzburg, or something.

Rust is not in Europe for fun, but business. This is a research trip. Rust has been commissioned to write a biggie this time: an Anglo/German/American co-production with theatrical release and world TV potential and video spinoff and fuck knows what else. Megabucks. Rust won't be getting the megabucks, of course, he never does. Rust will be on a flat fee, he always is. Probably he will not even get his full fee, which as usual is only payable on the First Day of Principal Photography, or St Nevercome's Day, as Bertolt Brecht called it. So Rust will get his cut of what is called the Development Money, which is a few lousy grand to write the draft screenplay, and the expenses for this Grand Tour of Little Known German Shitholes. He'll write the draft screenplay, after which they'll abort the whole production, or get another writer in, screw Rust somehow, anyway, by one of the many stratagems available to them.

So what's the story? What's this three-way co-production angle? Well, actually, it's rather neat. It's all about this young *English guy* who is all washed up in *Thatcher's England* so he takes this wonderful opportunity to explore his full potential in the *new vibrant Europe*, but what it turns out to be is a job selling encyclopædias on commission to *American service personnel* in and around the big bases in Bavaria. *Sex, ambition, politics, irony.* The English salesman as the new vagabond of Europe, poverty-stricken and pig-ignorant, despised by Kraut and Yank alike, but of course the hero will have a lot of *personal charm* to offset the ignorance and poverty bit so that we can have the *romantic angle* not only with the left-wing skinny but sexy proud contemptuous *German bint* but also with the *black American girl soldier* from the Deep South.

Rust can't imagine that any girl soldier, black or white, is going to want to spend more time talking to him than it takes to tell him to haul ass, so the American girl is probably going to have to be pure fantasy, straight out of Hemingway, why not, and none the worse for that. 'I will be your little rabbit. I will be your good girl.' Brilliant. Can't beat it. Why aren't *real* women like that?

The German girl, on the other hand ... well, Rust does pride himself he knows a thing or two about German girls ... women! Women! Sorry! Christ, that was a close one. The one that broke his heart before the one that's just broken his heart again was a German, um, thing, *and* left-wing, skinny, sexy, proud and contemptuous. A bit out of Rust's usual class, actually. The thing was, she said, German men with beards were nearly always sensitive arty intellectual types with leftish leanings; she hadn't been in Britain long enough to notice that British men with beards are as likely as not to be nightclub bouncers, all-in wrestlers, or even mass sex killers. By the time she did notice, it was too late. Rust had got his beard under the table, so to speak. She left him in the end, of course. They all leave him in the end. Leave him, high and dry, alone on a train full of foreigners, to be blown about the world by the four winds of the firmament; poor suffering Rust, who only wants to love and be loved and get a few bob together against his lonely old age ... who are the real wretched of the earth? Fucking freelance writers, that's who ...

God, his head hurts. Talk about dark nights of the soul. The thing about this research trip is that the producer and director have taken it all too seriously, and Rust is suffering in the cause of neo-realism. John, the young guy whose life Rust is plundering for the screenplay, travelled the hard way, Liverpool Street to Harwich and then the night ferry to the Hook of Holland and on by train to Cologne, then on another train along the Rhine to Wurzburg. So now Rust has to make the same trip so that he can get the authentic smell of it, while the producer and the director and John himself have flown ahead to Frankfurt – champagne all the way no doubt – snoring in their pits at this very moment no doubt in beautiful German bedrooms between lovely white smooth fragrant linen sheets, the bastards. Bastards. Bastards!

Cheer up, Ron boy. Always someone worse off than you. At least he's not still on that fucking ship. Ship of Death. Who was that? D. H. Lawrence? Was he a sailor boy at all? Not as far as Rust can recall. Ship of Shame. That was more like it. *The Last of England*. That fat, pissed young fellow from Liverpool, conducting his dispute with the Dutch barman with all the wit and aplomb for which his city is famed:
'I gave you ten, you blind bitch!'
'Five! Five! This blue one! It never go in the till! You try to cheat me, now you fuck off from my bar!'
'Ten, ten, I gave you ten, a brown one, like you, you piece of shit!'
'Listen, you English animal, I come over this bar I hit you so hard you wish you're dead!'

And so on. In the scuffle that followed, Rust was jolted into the arms of a thin, long-haired superannuated hippie type in his early thirties, old enough to know better, in Rust's view. This man gave Rust his views on the conditions of England and Europe as a whole, which were as follows: Bath used to be good, Bath, and Cheltenham, and Stroud, and all round there; he could count a hundred and thirty-five people just in Bath and round those parts where he could go and there would be a meal and a smoke and kisses and breakfast in the morning, and where was it all gone now, where did it go, could Rust tell him, no, because no one knew, it was all gone,

23

England was fucked, man, totally fucked, and everyone was getting on the boat, man, getting out any way they could, France, Spain, Germany, but Germany was a hard country, hard people there, *autobahn*, war machine, heavy place, but better than Maggie's Farm, right? Amsterdam, though, that was it, that was the real place, that was the best city in the world, best city in the world to beg in, any road.

'Any road?' said Rust, intrigued. 'Are you from Yorkshire?'

'Harrogate.'

'And you're a beggar. A sturdy Harrogate beggar.'

'Listen,' said the hippie. 'I'll make it easy on you. Ten guilders, and that's the whole deal, all over, what do you say? Five, then?'

'I've got no money to spare,' said Rust, looking at him hard.

That sort of material was no use to Rust. Not for a biggie with theatrical release. He supposed he might be able to plant it in a sodding short story or something, but what was the use of that? Who was going to pay Rust money for a sodding short story?

He felt strongly tempted to take the hippie by the throat and tell him a few grim facts about the literary life, and it must have shown in his eyes, because the hippie said hastily, 'OK, man, relax. I'll just take a cigarette off you and no hard feelings, right?'

From where Rust stood at the bar he could see three of the whores who worked the ferries sitting at a table having a drink and a giggle before starting the night's work. One of them was a big stocky woman who looked to be in her mid-forties, the others were in their early twenties. They could have been a mother and two daughters. They all had dark curly hair, and they seemed very close, as if they liked each other a lot.

The one that Rust liked best had a nice round face with plump cheeks. She had a bird tattooed on her shoulder. It looked like a seagull to Rust. Nice plump seagull. Nice plump girl. Woman, sorry. Nice, though. He wouldn't have minded having a sit down and a nice little chat with her in the interests of research. Just a chat. Rust had developed this sexual problem over the years; he could only shag women he loved and who loved him. Bloody inconvenient it was too. He could probably have fallen in love with this one if he hadn't had his heart broken so recently. Then he could have had a nice shag, which would have probably cheered him up no end. Ah, well. She turned and saw him looking at her and smiled. Nice smile. Rust smiled back and raised his glass of Aqvavit to her. Good stuff, Aqvavit.

He went up and stood on deck for a bit in the darkness and the rain, but there was nothing to see and the desolate loneliness of it all just made him start crying again like a prat . . . perhaps he could use this, have the hero motivated by a broken heart to leave England, somehow recycle self-pity into hard currency . . . Rust hated to waste anything.

He went back down to the bar and drank some more Aqvavit. The whores were dancing now, in the little circle of light that served as a disco floor. No one else was dancing. A circle of men stood outside the ring of light encouraging the dancing women to take their clothes off. Rust wandered away towards the gaming table where four drunk and mystified young English blokes were losing at blackjack to an expressionless, bespectacled young Dutch croupier at a startlingly brisk rate of knots. Pink puzzled faces, Neanderthal frowns, mouth-breathers to a man, trying and failing to follow the bewildering speed of the Dutchman's hands, eyes and brain, as the chips were raked in again and again in an emblematic icon of Sterling Entering the European Monetary System.

Gulls, whores, beggars, pedlars and freelance writers, surging into Europe on a sea of vomit, said Rust to himself rather grandly, and stumbled back to the bar for more Aqvavit.

The men were getting sorted from the boys now, and the women from the girls. Only two or three hours ago he had had to wriggle his way through a mass of backs three deep at the bar; now he enjoyed the barman's almost undivided attention. And over by the disco lights the older whore danced alone in the middle of the circle of men, and as Rust watched entranced, she hoicked up her skirt, lowered her knickers, and displayed a broad white bottom on which was tattooed a large and cheerful-looking dragon.

Hours later, he wandered alone, the only man left alive on the surface of the moon, dragging his feet through the thick red carpets, stepping over the silent, wrapped bodies of the sleepers on the floor, moving like a ghost or a sleepwalker along the long, shiny grey-and-cream corridors of the lower decks where the cabins were. And though he had a cabin booked, he could not bear to enter it. He knew that if he did he would only lie there curled around a pillow or a bottle, sobbing and calling her name.

Turning a corner he saw someone, a woman, coming out of one of the cabins, yawning, bending to adjust the ankle strap on her high-heeled shoes. It was one of the whores, the nice one with the plump face, the seagull-tattoo whore, Rust's whore. She turned and recognised him.
    'Hello. You're up late.'
    'Yea. You know. Can't sleep.'
    'You got a cabin, love?'
    'No,' he lied.
    'Can't really do anything if you haven't got a cabin, they're buggers on this boat, I shouldn't say that but they really are.' She had a South Wales accent.
    'Never mind,' said Rust. 'Night, then.'
    'Night.'

But later on, bewilderingly, she is in his cabin after all with a message that the production office has telexed through the money for a research shag for Rust, with a clear proviso that primary research officially outguns the love embargo. But the trouble is that the cabin is so small that Rust cannot work out how to achieve a juxtaposition of the crucial parts of their bodies: the bunks are so close on top of one another that two people could not possibly squeeze into one bunk, and the space between the bunks is so narrow that only one person could possibly stand in it. After a good deal of heaving and panting and one acute claustrophobic panic attack (Rust's, of course), she manages to squeeze, doubled up on her side, into

26

one of the bunks while Rust crouches in the opposite one; and she turns and smiles at him over her shoulder, her sweet plump shoulder with the seagull tattoo, and she hitches up her skirt and pulls down her knickers to expose an eloquently opulent backside which somehow also seems to be a Halifax Building Society Cashcard Screen with a dark horizontal slit into which Rust is invited to slide his Pan-European Smart Card.

Rust is appalled. It has all gone too far, he wants to get back into the Eighties, when he knew what was what, more or less; but she's telling him not to be so silly, just slip it in where the arrow indicates, after that everything'll be just the way he's always remembered it, just like a phonecard; and he slides it in and smells a sweet breeze from the Welsh valleys and yes, yes, after all it will be all right, he's going to be able to manage, and then, alarmingly, somehow her bottom is turning completely inside out, and it's all shiny and red and metallic on the inside and he doesn't like it, and now, oh God, the bunk above is crushing down slowly and inexorably on his head and that is even worse in fact it is desperate and he knows what it is to start to die and –

'*Bitte schön*! Excuse me, sir! Yes, please!'

Christ. Where is he? Who is he? He is . . . Rust. Ron Rust the writer. He's . . . in a train. And some old fart is shaking his shoulder and shouting in his face, bit bloody rude, bit bloody much, bit of a blinking liberty.

'Get off,' says Rust.

'Excuse me, sir you were shouting in your sleep. You were alarming the young lady.'

Rust grunts, blinks, and peers. Yes, there's a young lady in the corner, must have come in after he dozed off. More of a schoolgirl really. Violin case, navy mac, pony tail. Does look a bit alarmed.

'Bad dream,' says Rust. 'Awful dream. I was in a cabin, you see . . .'

He stops. They probably don't want to hear his dreams. Anyway, bad form, probably, telling pornographic nightmares to foreign strangers in long-distance International expresses. People do it all the time in Buñuel films, Rust does know that, but Rust has got into trouble before by taking Buñuel films as a model for social conduct in polite society.

'You speak English very well,' he says instead. 'Are you, ah, Dutch?'

'Do I *look* Dutch?' says the little man. Fuck knows, thinks Rust. He only said Dutch because everyone in Holland seems to speak English and everything else so brilliantly. This chap doesn't look particularly Dutch. Gold-rimmed spectacles, twinkly blue eyes for the use of, tweedy suit ending in sort of knickerbockers and walking boots. Could be English. Could be anything. J. R. Tolkien on speed, for all Rust knows. Well, it's keeping him awake and out of mischief.

'Not Dutch. *Deutsch*,' says the little man merrily, doing a sort of side-twinkle as well for the benefit of the sixth-form violinist.

'Oh ha ha ha very good ha ha,' goes Rust like the sycophantic berk he tries so hard not to be.

'And you, you are English, sir?'

'Absolutely,' says Rust.

'I was in England many years. As a prisoner of war, you know.

Rust pricks up his ears. Hello. Bit of the old background material here. Our hero could meet this guy on the train. Brilliant.

'Really?' he says. 'Like it, did you, England, like? All right, was it?' Not bad eh? Oh, old Rust can be fucking suave when he's in the vein.

'A beautiful place,' says Tolkien's twin brother, giving vent to a soulful sigh. 'Lake Windermere, that is where they were keeping the naval officers. So peaceful. Like holidays with pay!'

'Oh ha ha ha very good ha ha.'

'You know what they say to me?' He leans forward and gives Rust mega-twinkle from both lenses.

'What *do* they say to you?' asks Rust, falling pathetically into his Feed Man role, historic present and all.

'Überleutnant Wassermann, they are telling me, now the war is over for you. Now we are friends. This is in 1943, you understand. So charming? Yes? You know already in 1943 they are preparing North Atlantic Fleet, ready for when the

Russians are enemies again? So they need to make a friend of Überleutnant Wassermann, even though a week before, he commands a Nazi U-boat!'

He laughed merrily, wagging his finger and twinkling like the fairy on the Christmas tree. He had clearly told his story a good many time before, but Rust couldn't remember hearing anything quite like it. Shit. It was all the wrong sort of stuff for Rust's purpose. Now-it-can-be-told stuff. Thriller stuff. As-told-to stuff. Rust does most sort of stuff but he doesn't do that sort of stuff. Shit. What a waste of time. What a waste of stuff. What a waste of Rust.

'And are you thinking that I would co-operate with the enemy?'

'I don't know,' says Rust sulkily. 'Did you?'

'But of course I co-operated! Of course I co-operated!' The old bugger is patting me on the knee now! What next? 'Believe me, young man, we never had any quarrel with the British. Always we should have been friends, always we should have been together, we understand each other, German and English, you have German Royal Family, we should never have been enemies!'

Rust has never been keen on this particular line, but he is prepared to put up with a good deal from someone who is prepared to call him young man. The schoolgirl has her head down, reading her book. She is wrinkling her nose, probably in disgust at the old man's pre-Cambrian politics. She's probably some sort of Green terrorist herself, just the sort of person Rust should be researching for the skinny-but-sexy character, instead of this Teutonic Hobbit.

'And so for many years I am commanding Nato submarines, not officially of course, but in secret. Officially I am first a prisoner of war, then later I am interned. I understand it would be embarrassing to recognise me openly because I was a Nazi. Officially I am a problem, but among my English colleagues, politics was never something to worry about.'

Oh, God, thinks Rust, tell it to Jack Higgins, tell it to John le Carré, but for Christ's sake leave me out of it, OK?

The old man looks at his watch.

'Good, we make good time. Düsseldorf in five minutes. You are leaving the train at Köln?'

Rust admits it.

'Not long for you, then. For me, Nürnberg. First visit for many years.'

Rust looks out of the window. The flat lands race by. Nuremberg. Rallies. A bombing raid that went wrong.

'You know when I first came to Nürnberg?' says Wassermann. '1938. I was seventeen years old. I heard Hitler speak, you know. I was chosen from my village, as leader of the *Hitler-Jugendgruppe*.' He shakes his head, smiling. 'Fifty years ago.'

Rust wants very much to get his bottle of Aqvavit out of his bag and take a big swig of it. It's no good. He has to ask the old troll.

'So you believed in all that stuff then?'

Wassermann smiles and spreads his hands. 'Naturally, then. Why not?'

'But not now, eh?'

Wassermann leans forward. 'He was a great leader, stupid to deny this. Many fine ideas, he gave his nation work and bread and self-respect. You crossed on the Hook ferry? You liked what you see on that boat? You like what happens in Europe now? Listen to me, Hitler was a great leader, but like all the politicians he wanted to go too far. Yes?'

'You could say that, yes,' says Rust.

'Well, yes, of course. You have the same in England now, yes, Maggie Thatcher? They are all the same, yes? They all want to go a little too far, am I right?'

'Look,' says Rust. 'Maggie Thatcher hasn't started burning Jews yet, has she?'

Rust hardly sees the flicker on the old man's face: the smile is still there, the big twinkle, but all the warmth has gone out of it.

'And this is your first visit to Germany? I think you will find the natives very friendly.'

Rust gets a cigarette out and lights it. His hands are shaking a bit.

'You are staying in Köln?'

'No, just passing through.'

'So where are you staying, please?'

'Oh . . . Wurzburg. Bamberg. Uh . . . Augsburg, I think.'

'You will find these places very beautiful.'

'Oh, good,' says Rust.

'Permit me to point out that smoking is forbidden in this compartment.'

'Oh, sorry.' Shit. Yes, right. There's the sodding sign. He looks for somewhere to stub it out. No ashtray. He drops the stub on the floor and grinds it out with the heel of his Hush Puppy. When he looks up, they are both staring at him. The schoolgirl's mouth is twisted in disgust, or is that just his paranoid imagination?

'Yes, you will find these places very beautiful. Very clean, also, after England.'

'Really?'

'Yes, really. Very clean. But I think they will not be finding you very clean.'

Eh? *What* did he say?'

'Uh . . . what?'

'I am thinking that you would be wise to have a shower and a shave before you ask for your accommodation.'

'Well, yes,' says Rust. 'I was actually planning on that . . . been up all night, you know.' He is starting to feel very uncomfortable. The schoolgirl is staring at him as if he is some sort of disease.

'You are changing trains at Köln?'

'Um, yeah. Yes, I am.'

'You will have time to go to the cloakroom at Köln station. Go to the cloakroom and give yourself a good scrub down.' The old sod's tone has changed gradually. He sounds quite, well, sharp and stern.

'Right,' says Rust.

'Because you see you are smelling very bad. It is not pleasant.'

'What?'

'I am saying that you smell very bad. Your breath smells of spirits and your clothes smell of dirt and sweat and your feet smell of rotten meat. I am sorry to say this. But the young lady will confirm it.'

The schoolgirl stares at Rust in distaste. She doesn't need to say anything.

'I'm sorry,' says Rust. 'Athlete's foot.'

'You are an *athlete*?' The old man starts to chuckle in a sneering sort of way.

'You don't have to be an athlete to get athlete's foot,' Rust mumbles pathetically.

'*You* an *athlete*? I would not have your body for a *gift*!'

'Look,' says Rust. 'You're not in command of your fucking U-Boat now. We're all Europeans now, right?'

'You will leave this compartment now, please. Or I will call the guard and have you taken off the train. You have insulted and assaulted this young lady.'

And suddenly, relief floods Rust's body. It's OK. He's not back in a fucking nightmare. The old guy is crazy, that's all. U-boats, Nato, it was all fantasy. And there I was *apologising* for having athlete's fucking *foot*.

'Yeah, OK, no offence intended,' he says, standing up with a groan and pulling his bag down from the rack. 'I'll find another seat.'

At the door he pauses. He'll be leaving the schoolgirl with the old crazy.

'Uh, you think you should find another compartment as well?'

She stares back at him. Maybe she doesn't understand English. Ah well. He's made a gesture.

The next compartment is not only completely empty, it is a smoking compartment as well. Brilliant! Rust sinks back, sprawling across several seats, gets his Aqvavit out and has a good swig, and lights up. There. That's better. No one here to object to his stubble and his breath and his sweat and his foot. He's warm, dry and smoking, and before too long he'll be pissed as well. It's not perfect, but Rust has known worse times. Shame about the old Kraut. Not Jack Higgins stuff at all, as it turned out, but still not Rust stuff. Too far from the spine of the narrative, no set-up or pay-off, just a bit of life, really. Rotten bloody shame. Ah well.

And the train rolls on over the flat lands, carrying Rust deeper and deeper into the heart of Europe.

InfoTech Centre Memorandum No. 3

MEMORANDUM NO. 3

From: Central Direction
To: All personnel with clearance level two and above
Subject: data viruses

1. The problem

The problem is that infection of software and hardware by data viruses has now reached epidemic status. The epidemic is relatively mild in this country to date but transatlantic experience would suggest that it is firmly established, it is going to multiply exponentially during the next three years, and that at present there is no reliable cure. The only option open to us at present is to practise strict data hygiene at all times and to be constantly alert for Trojan horses. And the moose moose moose moose let us never forget about the moose oh my God here he comes now no false alarm I was only kidding.

2. What is a data virus?

It's just a little bug put into your system by a systems saboteur, or passed on to you by another data virus victim who doesn't even know that he/she is infected. You are probably harbouring at least two or three data viruses right now. So am I. Data viruses can cause anything from minor irritation to total mental breakdown and brain death. The analogy (often invoked) with AIDS is not quite

(more)

accurate. A more correct analogy might be with the whole spectrum of sexually transmitted infections and mooserot mooserot mooserot moose juice rotting the central nervous system of your WP repeat after me I practise data hygiene ol' moose won't get me no sir!

3. When they got bored with simply hacking

In the old days, in the days of Robin Hood and Merrie England, the hackers just wanted to hack into the system, which simply means breaking the security of anything from minis up to mainframes, and as everything gradually got hooked up, kids were finding that they could hack into the local Sainsburys and finish up breaking into the Pentagon, without ever leaving their bedrooms in Milton Keynes. Classic hackers were content to leave their signatures in a sort of Kilroy Was Here spirit: graffiti artists of the small screen, so to speak. An example:

The deputy manager of your local bank will load his spreadsheet program and instead of getting his usual friendly message that Spreadspeed One is Ready to Run, he will be invited to spread the cheeks of his arse and get ready to bite the pillow because Shirtlifters International are coming to town and they are looking for YOU.

That sort of thing. Inconvenient, but relatively harmless. See 'Dirty Faxes'.

The game moved on from this to the more sophisticated game of modifying the (already broken) system so that when the initial loophole was closed (the wound was dressed, stitched, cauterised, and treated with antibiotics) and the system reset to its normally secure state, the virus went on working inside. One way of doing this was to arrange matters so that the security system was repeatedly broken when certain parts of the normal software were activated. This operation is called planting a Trojan Horse.

(more)

In the case of this document we suspect that the virus is triggered by the phrase 'all personnel with clearance levels two and above'.

they come in the they come in the night and get into your brain and hide there they hide in your brain and then they spill out in the program or flop out of the fax like long dirty tongues.

Christine would you read that back to me please?

Thank you Christine. This document is almost certainly dv positive.

There is no need for panic. Follow the data hygiene regime prescribed on page 406 of the handbook.

Erase the disc and shred the printout.

(ends)

OK fine Christine now no one need ever know. It was a dirty infected document but it is gone for ever. Flop out of the fax like long dirty tongues. I hate that word flop. You're sure you erased the file and shredded the printout?

Yes sir.

OK what's next?

The campus thing, sir.

Oh yeah good that's very traditional and nice with gentle irony and everything . . . are we having any problems with that?

Tendency to break out into confessional italics, sir, but I think we've ironed that one out now.

You better. OK. Let her roll.

Ready to run, sir.

You absolutely sure you erased that other thing?

(ends)

Dirty Faxes

Stephen St John Coke decides he needs a haircut, right? He goes down Jermyn Street to his usual place, but it's shut. Just as he's about to hail a cab and go back to his flat, he sees a striped barber's pole down a little alley, and he thinks, well, why not? A haircut is a haircut, and perhaps he's been stuck in a rut for too long so far as the old back and sides are concerned. He pushes the door which offers a slight and satisfying resistance and prompts a reassuringly traditional mechanical sort of bell.

As soon as he is inside he realises that he has made a mistake. Though most of the clients appear to be men, two of them are young women, and all the staff appear to be female. Stephen is a bit fussy about whose fingers are allowed to fiddle with his ears and the nape of his neck. Still, he's in now, and he's going to tough it out.
    The woman is about thirty years old, stockily built, her own hair 'a mass of carefully-contrived brassily metallic curls'.
    'We'll try not to keep you too long, dear, would you like a book?'
    'Yes, please,' says the novelist. 'Have you got War and Peace*?'*
    'No, sorry, we haven't got that one. Woman's Own*?'*
    'Forget it,' he says haughtily.
    'You look a bit down, dear,' she says. 'What is it? Weather? Love life?'
    'Existential boredom,' he confesses.

'Mm,' she says thoughtfully. 'You could always have a wank.'

'I am too proud to wank.'

'Ooh, are you? That's funny – we've got another gentleman down there under the drier, he's just the same about that, Mr Darcy his name is, do you know him at all?'

Stephen St John Coke begins to panic.

'Look,' he says. 'What is all this? Am I in a dream?'

'Yes,' she says. 'You are, and there's fuck all you can do about it, you toffee-nosed tautologiser, you carefully-contrived brassily metallic misogynist, because this is my dream. My shop, my dream, Mr Too Proud To Wank St John Coke!'

'How . . . how did you know my name?' stammers the novelist. Proud he may be, but not vain in the ordinary sense, and though his books are well known he avoids interviews and does not allow his photograph to appear on dust-jackets.

'Oh, I know all about you,' she says grinning. 'I even know you like the smell of my hole.'

All the blood drains from his cheeks. How could she say a thing like that? How could he be hearing it? But it is there, it has been spoken, it is out in the open, and now it has been said he knows that it is true, that what has been holding him here despite his fear, his distaste, his aristocratic nose-crinkling hauteur, has been the overpoweringly rich stench of . . . well . . . not to put too fine a point on it, fresh cunt juice that surrounds this otherwise irredeemably vulgar person. Hyperventilating, he fumbles furiously with his fly-buttons, but before he can release his tormented Tommy Rogers, he falls forward in a dead faint, and they drag him out the back and give him a good kicking, and serve the bugger right.

Stephen St John Coke lets the thin slippery sheets of thermal paper slide out of his hand onto his rich dark shiny mahogany desk. He is trying very hard to stop shaking and whimpering. His room is quiet. His clock ticks melodiously in the corner. His cat Belloc lies on the back of the leather Chesterfield in the window alcove, fast asleep and snoring slightly. His antique Persian and Kashmir rugs glow softly in the lamplight. His pen lies on the leather blotter. His pencils, sharp and scented, huddle upright in their dark blue Chinese jar. His thick marbled notebooks are filled with line after line in his elegant and legible italic hand. His endearingly old-fashioned Underwood office typewriter is for emergencies only: his manuscripts are typed for him by an agency. There are his pictures: Braque, Gwen John, Fuseli. And there is his fax machine.

Apart from his telephone, the fax machine is the only thing in the room that looks under thirty years old. It sticks out like a sore thumb, and Stephen St John Coke hates and fears it. He never wanted one in the first place, but he found himself the recipient of an offer he could not refuse: to write, for a fee of $1_____, a screenplay of *Le Rouge et Le Noir* for the world-famous director_____. The great director was charmed to find a writer who didn't even use a typewriter, let alone a Mac or a Wang, but insisted that the Italian money bought Coke a fax machine, and despite Coke's resistance, it was all done in a couple of hours, and there the thing is now, sitting in the corner watching him with its little green eye. And God knows what it's planning to do next.

The technician who installed it was very kind and patient, and quite anthropomorphic in his tutorial instructions: he showed the novelist how his fax machine could call up another fax machine, and how the two machines would shake hands with each other for a few moments to find out if they were compatible, and then if they were, the second fax machine would shyly declare itself ready to receive whatever message Coke's machine cared to lay on it. And *vice versa*, of course.

'You don't even have to be there, that's the beauty of it. They can call each other up and talk and fax each other in the middle of the night while you're asleep if that's the way you want it,' the man said, and Coke was obscurely touched to think of all the quiet faithful fax machines squatting on desks in dark and silent offices long hours after everyone else had gone home, their little green lights glowing, calling each other up and shaking hands, finding out if they were compatible and then faxing each other quietly in the darkness.

And at first he did like it, he did like playing with his new toy. He badgered his acquaintances to buy faxes, so that he could fax them letters and receive their replies within minutes, wherever in the world they or he might be. There was something a touch fanciful about this, even wishful: there are few who wish to communicate so urgently with Stephen St John Coke, and fewer still whom he is eager to contact. He is not, in his own opinion, misanthropic, but there is that about him which discourages intimacy. He lives alone, and prefers to do so. He was married, but now he is separated from his wife. She was much younger than he, it was not a success, he loved her as well as he was able, he believes, but she was restless and unhappy, and as hot for – well, it was not a success, and when she left, it was at his request.

He has not repeated the experiment. He has female friends, of course he has, but he does not, at present or for the foreseeable future, feel inclined to invade their bodily orifices; nor is he tormented by more generalised erotic yearnings, and even if he were, he is, like Mr Darcy, too proud to . . . no! He will not allow himself to be constructed by this vile discourse which spews out of the little green-eyed monster! He will not consider it. It has nothing to do with him, nothing! And yet . . . and yet . . .

How did it all begin? Where did it start to go wrong? Belloc has been suspicious of the fax machine from the start. One day, when Coke had only had the thing a week, he went out to buy a packet of Earl Grey and came back to find Belloc in a desperate wrestling match with several yards of shiny printout, merely a lengthy memo from the great director____ ____, but to Belloc an alien intruder squirming out of the green-eyed fax like a snake through the letterbox, with Belloc alone in the house to repel the invader. Stephen St John Coke laughed aloud then, laughed his rare creaking laugh, laughed aloud at his brave and perceptive cat. But Belloc was right. It was no laughing matter.

It was all right at first. The thing was surprisingly easy to manipulate. _____ _____ sent memos to Stephen St John Coke, and Stephen St John Coke sent memos and outlines and little scenes to Paris and New York and Amsterdam, wherever the great director happened to be. It made him feel efficient, in tune, even modern; it made him feel like a man who knew how to live in the late twentieth century. He has become attuned to its little sounds: the small, barely audible click which means his machine is shaking hands with another, and which precedes the long low moaning sound his fax machine makes when it is being faxed, the sound that Coke has come to dread, the sound that accompanies the excretion of a long slippery sheet of whatever they have thought up now to torment him with.

His agent was delighted when he heard about Coke's fax machine, and sent him something on it nearly every day: reviews, cuttings, contracts, copies of letters, usually accompanied by a note from his agent's secretary B_____ in her louche scrawl: 'R_____ thought that this would amuse you. B_____.' Or even simply: 'Here's another of those things. B.' This he did find mildly disconcerting. He has always had proper typed letters before, typed by B_____, but (he assumes) dictated as well as signed by R_____. And B_____, when Coke has encountered her on his rare visits to the agency, has always seemed a demure and pretty young woman, polite and friendly without being forward, given to lowering her long-lashed bright brown eyes when she is being spoken to. Her typing has always been impeccable. It is a little disquieting to find that she has the handwriting of a voluptuary.

Next came the phantom phone calls. Coke's machine is a modest affair as fax machines go; it does not possess, as some other fax machines possess, a built-in handset. So that when, after a couple of weeks, it started to ring like a telephone, Stephen St John Coke was hard put to it to know what to do. The little panel that carried the VDU and told him what was going on said:

OPERATOR CALLING! OPERATOR CALLING! PLEASE RESPOND!

But Coke did not know how to respond. On one or two

occasions he actually picked his machine up and turned it round and round, trying to prise it open like a giant oyster and force it to yield up its secrets. No use, of course. After a dozen or so rings it would stop, and the VDU would tell him: INCOMPLETE: MESSAGE ABORTED. INFORMATION CODE 420. PLEASE TRY AGAIN. But Coke did not, does not know what to try, and now, when his fax machine rings, he huddles furtively in the corner, trying to pretend it isn't happening, hoping the phantom caller will go away and leave him alone.

And now this. It's not the first, but it is the worst. The others were briefer, and though quite often threatening, were less personal, less intimate, less . . . *knowing*. There were newspaper cuttings, nearly all of them about men called Stephen Coke or Cook, nearly all of them brief reports from the criminal courts, detailing the petty offences of these other Cooks and Cokes: fraud, deception, theft, drunkenness, gross indecency, and so on. Not very amusing, really. But nothing, surely, to worry about. One of his friends had decided to tease and tantalise him out of his habitual solemnity, that's all. Except that Coke can't think of any friend of his who would be inclined, or could be bothered, or – and here's the rub – *cares* enough about him to research and perpetrate such an elaborate practical joke.

It's not just cuttings. Often when he hears the little click and then the low moan and tiptoes to the fax machine to see what is seeping out of it, he finds it's another of those advertisements. Somehow he seems to have been put on the fax machine equivalent of a mailing list of a particularly inappropriate and embarrassing kind. Hardly a day passes when he is not offered *services* (he supposes he would have to call them), services he has never solicited, does not require, would not appreciate, and in some cases has never heard of. Persons of both sexes fax their availability to visit him in the privacy of his own home in order to administer anything from verbal abuse to colonic irrigation.

Then there are the business faxes, most of them from mail order companies demanding money for goods Coke has never ordered: women's underwear, high-heeled shoes, motor-cycling attire, enuresis pads, artificial limbs, and so on. Some of them threaten legal action or worse. Coke is bravely ignoring them. All that has happened so far is that the firms write again and again in more and more offensive terms. Coke can keep his countenance in the face of that sort of thing.

But this one is something else again. It is not about any old Stephen Coke or Cook: it is about him, Stephen St John Coke the novelist. And though its prose style makes him shudder, the content indicates a disturbing knowingness about him. He does, for example, get his hair cut in Jermyn Street. But that is something anyone might guess about him. His fondness for Tolstoy is a matter of public record. 'Toffee-nosed' runs off him like water off a duck's back. 'Misogynist' is neither here nor there. But 'Tautologiser' hits him where it hurts. He is furious with his tormentor, and furious with himself. How could he have let that phrase slip by, how could his editor have missed it? Even R____ his agent could normally be relied upon to murmur a few words about something as gross as 'brassily metallic'. And this in his new novel, whose official publication date, he suddenly remembers, is not until next month. This vile person, whoever she is – he just *knows* it's a woman – must have got hold of a proof copy somehow.

But even that could not explain Tommy Rogers away. Not even Lalage had known about Tommy Rogers. Only Hugh Fitzwilliam and Edwin Gore, who had been his best friends and shared his dormitory at preparatory school, know that Coke's John Thomas was known to its owner as Tommy Rogers. Though even Hugh and Edwin could hardly know that this is what Coke still calls his unsociable fifty-year-old phallus. They all had special names, Coke now remembers. Hugh's was called Willy Wood, and Edwin's was called Dickie Dangle, a misnomer if ever there was one, for Dickie was a sturdy thrusting little chap, forever straining lustily against the constricting embrace of Edwin's thick grey flannel shorts. What happy days they were! Life seemed so simple then. Coke's face feels odd and he realises that he is smiling.

But this won't do. The dirty faxes can't be anything to do

with Hugh or Edwin. Hugh is MP for Borehamwood, and Edwin an eminently respectable solicitor in Scarborough. And Willy Wood and Dickie Dangle, Coke is sure, have long since declined into a respectable and inactive middle age, as has Tommy Rogers. So *who is doing this to him*?

Coke hears a tiny click. Belloc opens his eyes and puts his ears back, swearing softly to himself. The fax machine's little green eye flickers. It is shaking hands with someone. Then with a little groan, it starts to squeeze out paper. His heart thumping, Coke stumbles over to the machine. He sighs with relief as he recognises B____'s sprawling hand: 'Have you seen this one?'

It's a review of his new novel. From the *New London Literary Journal*. The title of the review is 'The Emperor's Old Clothes'. It is not a good review. It is a bad review. It is a clever, vicious, and brutally unfair review by someone called V. Z. Savage, a critic unknown to Coke. The general gist of the argument, amply supported by quotation, is that Coke, like several of his famous contemporaries, is played out, that he has given us the mixture as before, a mixture that has no meaning or relevance either to the world we live in or to the House of Fiction. His language is exhausted and derivative. His characters (yes, Coke is still fiddling about with the comically outmoded concept of character) are like bits of limp cardboard. His epithets are tautologous as well as being misogynistic. Every time a woman appears on the page, you can bet she'll have a mass of carefully-contrived . . .

Coke can bear no more of this. But wait – B____ has scribbled another message at the end. For a moment his eyes are too blurred with angry tears to read it. He dabs impatiently at them with his fine linen blue and white spotted handkerchief. There. That's better. He tears off the fax and peers at the last two lines.

'Never mind, Stephen. How would you like to sit on my tits and flop those big balls in my face?'

It is some moments before Coke can breathe, let alone speak.

He picks up the telephone and dials his agent's number. Trying not to gabble, he asks R____ if he has read the review and if he can decipher B's handwritten note at the end of the fax.

'What fax?' says his agent. 'We haven't sent you anything today, have we?'

'Yes, a viciously insulting review from the *New London Literary Journal*!'

'Hang on, Stephen,' says R____. Coke can hear him asking B____ if she has faxed him anything, and he hears her saying no.

'She's lying!' he says.

'Hold on, Stephen. Where did you say this review came from?'

'The *New London Literary Journal*.'

'There isn't any such thing, Stephen. There's the *Literary Journal* and the *London Review of Books* . . . you sure you got it right?'

Coke can feel the cold sweat running down his back. Of course. Of course there is no such thing as the *New London Literary Journal*. He knew that all along. But the fax had his agent's ID on it, and B____'s handwritten note.

'Could you just ask B____ if she sent me a little note?'

There is a pause at the other end.

'She says she doesn't think so. What did it say?'

'Er . . . doesn't matter.'

'Shall I put her on?'

'No, no . . . d'you know, I think I must have dreamed the whole thing? Yes, I dropped off after lunch and then woke up with the very firm idea that I had to ring you about something. You're quite right. There wasn't any fax at all.'

It doesn't sound very convincing to Coke. Nor, clearly, to his agent.

'Everything all right, is it, Stephen?'

'Yes, yes, good God, yes! Fine!'

'Well, er . . . take it easy, Stephen.'

'Right. Sorry to be a . . . well . . . goodbye then.'

Take it easy? How can he take it easy? He is sitting there with the fax in his hand, with V. Z. Savage's merciless review of his new novel, and B____'s even more distressing obscene proposition. Sit on her tits? He has never allowed himself to think about her breasts at all, and if he were to think about them, that is what he would call them, breasts, not tits. He might be a misogynist but he is not a vulgarian. Flop his big balls in her face? How disgusting! He should have taken a strong line with R____ and had her dismissed from the agency. What could be going on in the girl's head? Quite clearly she has made up the review, just as she made up that ridiculous story about the hairdresser. Foul, filthy creature! Or . . . or was that perhaps a little harsh? He remembers her face on his visits to the agency: sweet, demure, rather gentle and submissive. The character of Ophelia comes into Coke's mind. She went mad, and uttered all kinds of obscenities in her innocent derangement. If B____ is deranged, perhaps it is not her fault. Perhaps she needs help. Perhaps she needs skilled psychiatric treatment.

But even so. How could she make up such utter filth? The smell of her hole? My balls in her face? Tommy Rogers?

And Stephen St John Coke howls aloud, causing his good cat Belloc to leap off the Chesterfield in terror and vanish into the night. B____ could not possibly have known about Tommy Rogers. No one could have made that filth up but Stephen St John Coke himself. And the other thought that floods into his mind with utter conviction is that more than anything in the world he would like to sit on B____'s tits and flop his big balls into her face.

Now it is four in the morning. Belloc has not returned. The novelist sits in his dark study, trembling, his eyes on the single small green eye that stares back at him. And then, from somewhere deep inside the guts of his fax machine, a telephone bell begins to ring, and it is ringing for him.

French Baby

One trouble with the coffee shop of the Columbia-President on West 46th, Alice decided, was that nobody in it except her seemed to speak American. The staff looked, sounded and behaved like a quarrelsome Mexican family, and the clients were all English, German, Japanese, and every kind of dumb, helpless European you could think of.

'You want English muffin, corn muffin, or Danish?'

'Danish muffin, darling? Two Danish muffins, please.'

'Not Danish *muffin*. *Danish*. You want muffin, or you want Danish?'

'Um . . . what was the other thing?'

And so on.

Another drawback was the view. West 46th linked Broadway and 8th Avenue, and 8th Avenue was all-night male porno movies, cheap booze shops, winos, crazies, and dropouts. But this time in the morning – eleven already and still the writer hadn't showed – the shadows had moved off the wide shallow steps of the 46th Street Theater, and several bums had settled for the day with their bottles and brown bags, rolling up their pants to let the sun get to their sores. Alice was from Vermont herself and still noticed things like that.

The staff were now arguing in Spanish about who should take the garbage out, while a miserable English family waited patiently to gain their attention. Abandoning the bums to their sores and bottles, Alice decided to show the way.

'Could somebody bring some more coffee here?' she said in her clear, rather harsh voice. All the Mexicans turned round, and Alice stared them down until the thin, middle-aged woman, the one who finally got to do all the work, sighed theatrically and went for the jug. When she came back, Alice said thanks and gave her a nice smile.

'Enjoy it,' said the woman, indicating clearly that she herself personally had not enjoyed anything at all for a very long time.

Alice had, since February, spent too much time waiting for the writer in the coffee shop of the Columbia-President. Of course he would have to choose a hotel with psychotic service and a view of decomposing flesh. Grant Green had personally offered him a lovely apartment in the Upper East Seventies, but the writer had insisted on the theatre district because, he said, he needed to feel part of what was going on. The real reasons (Alice privately thought) were that he was too lazy to make his own bed, too mean to pay cab fares, and too scared to ride the subway. The writer was called Kevin Crowe, and Alice was having an affair with him.

This affair was extremely convenient for Green, Macfarlane (the production company for which Alice worked – first desk on the left as you go in), it had been an important learning experience for Alice, and the general opinion was that it was the only thing that had any chance of holding the writer together.

'He'd be falling apart with you, Alice,' they all said, and she could readily imagine bits of Kevin Crowe left abandoned in dim bars, under rumpled beds, in the kitchens of lobster restaurants; in all of which places he had mislaid metaphorical bits of himself – notes for the director, hundred-dollar *per diem* checks, and vital show-saving rewrites, until Alice had taken him in hand. Now it was crisis time. They were three days into previews, a week from press night, and Kevin's play was not getting across. It was getting polite respect, and that is a terrible thing for a new show to get. People were having an interesting evening, and Grant Green was hitting the panic button. At thirty-five dollars a ticket people wanted a transcendental experience or a woolly-assed good time, preferably both. What they didn't want was an interesting evening.

Even Alice, who loved and believed in the play, had to

acknowledge that last night, playing to New Yorkers in a number one Broadway theatre, Kevin's play, for all its wit and sensitivity, had felt, somehow, wispy and reticent, kind of invalid-ish, scared of itself, kind of, well . . . British.

And that was nothing to what Grant Green thought. Grant had grabbed her at the intermission. 'Get the writer up to my office as soon as it goes down. This show is bleeding to death, we got to get it on the table fast.'

So, Grant's office: where no matter how many people showed up, there were always enough oatmeal sofas. Waiting for Grant. Grant always showed late. Why not? It was his office. When Alice had her own office, she would show late. There was Mo Muscadet the director with his cruel black beard offset by mild blinky eyes; there was Larry Shell the production manager in what looked like his second clean shirt of the evening; there was Kevin Crowe the writer, dressed as usual as if on Welfare checks; and there was Alice, the writer's keeper.

Ideas had been tossed into the ball park to be kicked around. Mo felt the energy was draining in the second act. The star had nothing to play with, so she was playing desperation. Larry felt that no one was going for the character of Silas; Silas was not coming out and grabbing us, he was laying down and dying. Kevin had turned his wounded eyes to Alice and Alice had said she had to go along with Larry on that one. (Yes, she loved the writer, but one day millions of dollars would depend on her professional judgement, and that was her professional judgement.)

Mo told Kevin, 'I have to say this, Kevin, I feel it's in the writing. You gotta write Silas his balls back. Write him his balls back, you'll have hats on the goddam stage.'

Alice nerved herself for Kevin's outburst. One day millions of dollars would depend on her professional judgement, but tonight her job would be to pick up the pieces of a battered British writer.

But Kevin had been uncharacteristically quiet. Sappingly, exhaustingly, finally frighteningly quiet, he waited until he had drawn them all into his silence, his clenched stillness.

Then:

'My little girl's dog got knocked down by a car last night.'
He nodded slowly three times, his eyes like round black holes
in his pale face. 'That's been my day. That's been my shit of
a day. That's what's on my mind today, Mo. That is very
important to me, Mo, and what you say about Silas is not
very important to me.'

The silence that followed this had been almost as long as
the one that preceded it. The three Americans had stared at
one another helplessly. Little girls? Dogs? What was all this?
Had the writer flipped, or was it some new kind of British
humour?

Eventually Mo had said, 'Yeah, sure, Kevin, but in the
present situation . . .' and tailed off hopelessly. Larry had
opened his mouth and shut it a couple of times, and suddenly
got up and gone out of the office, perhaps to phone for men
with white coats. Kevin had sat on calmly. There was
something suicidally splendid about him, this skinny contemptuous little man on whom so many people's dollars
depended, and who treated them with such disdain, and who
was surely about to be personally chewed into little bits by
Grant Green of Green, Macfarlane. Then the door opened and
Grant Green was there.

'Kevin, I just heard about your little girl. Don't say a thing,
kid, words can't express. Get yourself around a good steak,
worries. Alice: look after this man, he's very precious to me.'
And Grant Green, astonishingly, one muscular arm round
each of their shoulders, had propelled the writer and the
writer's keeper into the elevator that would take them forty-
four floors down into the teeming New York night.

The teeming New York night was one thing the writer liked
about New York, despite his assertions to the contrary. He
liked to shout peevishly for port in anxious new restaurants
where they'd never heard of it; he liked to drink bourbon in
bars where big men in aprons refused to serve mixed drinks;
he liked to thread his wavering provocative way down 8th
Avenue and buy his bottle where the bums bought theirs . . .
Alice didn't want to think any more about the teeming New

York night. She had got the writer home: Green, Macfarlane's property was still in one piece.

The malevolent gang who staffed the coffee shop had found a new interest. A handsome man of about thirty in a brilliantly white open-necked shirt had come in from the street. Perched lightly on a bar stool as if for flight, he was asking with considerable charm and many gestures for *lait chaud* and they were pretending not to understand him. They were pretending not to understand him because it amused them, because they were mean Mexicans, and because none of them wanted to heat the milk.

The Frenchman was not put out. He seemed to enjoy the challenge, including everybody in his game. He called over to Alice, '*Je suis Français, mademoiselle. Parlez-vous Français? Ah, dommage!*'

Alice grinned.

'What we got here,' said the woman, pointing to the menu. 'Milk. Hot coffee. Tea. No hot milk.'

The Frenchman explained, in French, but with a breathtakingly elegant mime, how to take cold milk, heat it in a saucepan, and pour it into a jug. He drank the imaginary *lait chaud*. It was delicious! He kissed his fingers. He spread his hands, waiting.

'No hot milk,' said the woman.

'No hot meelk?'

'No hot meelk. You want coffee?'

'*Non.*'

'You want tea?'

'*Non.*'

'You want a cold meelk?'

'*Non*. I want a hot meelk.'

'Listen,' said the thin woman, with savage intensity. 'No hot meelk. Hot meelk only for baby.'

The Frenchman rolled his eyes, smiled bewitchingly across at Alice, then turned back to the woman in triumph. 'I am a baby.'

'You're a baby?'

'Yes,' he said solemnly. 'I am a French baby.' There was a long silence, then the woman began to laugh. The Frenchman began to laugh. All the Mexicans began to laugh and tell each other about the French baby, and the woman went in the kitchen to heat the milk.

Alice sipped her coffee. Eleven-ten. At six she had left the writer's bed (stepping in an abandoned Swiss cheese and cole-slaw sandwich), taken a cab across town to her own apartment, showered, fed her cats and her plants, checked the figures for Friday night, done her yoga exercises, and jogged back across town in time to shower again and be at her desk by eight. At five minutes after eight Grant Green had flung the door open.

'Alice! In here!' Alice went in there.

'I now find,' said Grant Green with some passion, 'that that asshole of a British writer screwed our meeting not because his fucking daughter got run down by a car last night, but because his fucking daughter's fucking *dog* got run down by a car. Is that right, Alice?'

'That's right, Grant,' said Alice.

'Asshole,' said Grant Green. 'That man is very precious to me, Alice, but he is an asshole. Ass-*hole*.'

'Kind of a precious asshole, right?' said Alice.

Grant Green looked at her very hard. Grant Green was said to have the smallest eyes in show business.

'Now what I want you to do, Alice, is get over to the Columbia-President, get the asshole out of bed, and tell him from me that he is not in this town to tell us sob stories about his goddam daughter's *dog*, he is in this town to earn the fucking *per diems* he gets every day, and do some rewrites for those poor assholes on stage to work with. I want good product on my desk by noon, tell the asshole, or he can get the next plane out of town. Do you think you could do this for me, Alice?'

Alice said she thought she could do that. She went back to the writer's room, got him out of bed, pushed him under the shower, found his clothes, and put a pen in his hand. And came down here.

The woman came out of the kitchen with the hot milk. She was walking like a young girl.

'OK,' she said. 'Hot milk for French baby.'

The French baby kissed his hand to her, and lifted the hot milk high to include the whole coffee shop in his happiness. Then he smiled directly across at Alice, smiled such a brilliant, sad, understanding French smile that she was hardly aware that Kevin had come in and slipped, groaning softly, into the bench opposite her.

'Coffee,' said the writer with his hands over his eyes. One of the Mexicans brought him coffee. He sipped in silence. He looked bad. He didn't seem to have any rewrites with him. He looked like one badly burned-out writer.

'Good news,' he said eventually, smiling very tentatively as if he might do himself damage. He took his hands away from his eyes and looked at her. Oh, yes. There was still that. But Alice steeled herself. She was working for Green, Macfarlane, and she would still be working for Green, Macfarlane, please God, when the writer had been hauled off back to Europe.

'You got the rewrites?'

He looked down at the table. He looked up at her face. Was there something childishly cunning in his smile?

'The dog's going to be OK.'

'Oh, that's wonderful,' said Alice flatly.

'Yeah. That's all right, that is. Took me more than an hour to raise anyone, but I did in the end, and he's going to be OK. That's the main thing. Right?'

'You haven't done the rewrites?'

'Give me a little while, Alice.' Christ. Didn't he know how many people were waiting on those rewrites? Didn't he know Alice's job was on the line here? Maybe he knew all right. Like the Mexicans knew about the milk.

'I was bad last night,' he said.

'You were.'

'Tell me.'

'Well,' said Alice. 'When I got you back to the room you were pretty wonderful for a little while. You said you were going to show me the pleasures of a long slow English bath to relax the harsh rhythms of my ruthlessly efficient lifestyle. And when you got me in there you said some pretty nice things.'

'What did I say?'

'You told me my toes were like little innocent pink brides.'

'Then what?'

'Oh, it was all downhill after that. We got to bed but you passed out with a Swiss cheese sandwich on your chest.'

'I remember that sandwich,' he said, and then, 'I don't deserve you.'

'This is true.' She was beginning to believe it.

'Got a pencil?' he said. 'Rewrite coming.'

For a while Kevin was silent, looking through the Mexican woman, who was appraising him with the critical stare of a long-time hangover expert. Then he began.

'Silas wakes up suddenly. He turns to the two women and smiles. Hello, Liddie, he says. And then, hello, Jane. You know, I was thinking about a time, a good time, a time long ago. When we were by a river. We were all sitting by a river and we had wine, and we had cheese, and the sun was shining. I was there, and you were there, Liddie, and Jane was there. Nidderdale, says Liddie. Nidderdale, says Silas. That was a good time, wasn't it?'

Alice scribbled furiously, not daring to interrupt. This was it. This was the rewrite that was going to save the play.

'And we were sitting there, drinking the wine, watching the water, hearing the grass move in the wind. You had your shoes off, Liddie. I remember your toes . . . like ten little innocent pink brides.'

Alice wrote the words. She was in the play. Her little innocent pink brides were in the play.

Kevin, as Silas, went on.

'And then, it was like a sign. This single huge bird . . . a heron, came from very far away down the river . . . slow and silent, all along the river, as if it were blessing the river with the slow beat of its wings, and the wine, and the water, and you, Liddie, and Jane, and me.

'A long pause. Then Silas says: I'm going to write a new song about that, Liddie. And you're going to be in it, and I'm going to be in it, and Jane's going to be in it.

'He stops. There's something different about the quality of their listening. Something's gone wrong. Then, after a long silence, Liddie says: Silas, you *wrote* that song. You wrote that song five years ago. Another long pause, for the pain to register. Then he says: Oh . . . doesn't matter. End of rewrite.'

And as she scribbled the last words, Alice felt a little rush of hope and optimism, like fresh water running over her throat and wrists. As if she'd taken her brains out and run them under a cool shower. Maybe, just maybe, all the scenes, all the bars, all the failed sex, all the hassle had been worth it. They had a show now, and she was in it.

'Coffee,' said Kevin to the Mexican woman.

'Oh, Kevin,' said Alice. 'That's it. That's the whole thing.'

It wasn't really the whole thing, she knew that, but it was something. It was in a way sort of cute, English cute, and it still had that kind of weak wistful British charm, but that was what she liked about Kevin anyway. And yes, yes, it was even money that he had simply recycled some old song of his, as Silas had, but he had done it with fastidious skill, like an invisible mend, he had made the loop, he had got her off the hook with Grant Green, and best of all he had slipped his love for her right in there. His secret message to her.

And look at him now: all crumpled and blotchy and ratty-looking. She suddenly felt very tender towards him. She put her hand over his and smiled at him.

The writer smiled back, a funny twisty little smile.

'Yeah,' he said eventually. 'I thought that was just about the right kind of *Reader's Digest* slop to light up the dollar signs. Glad to be of service to you all.'

Through all the buzzing in her head Alice could hear the Frenchman telling the Mexicans all about Paris and why he had to have hot milk. Her eyes were burning. She turned abruptly away from the writer. Outside the window the bums were passing around a bottle of Night Train, brand leader amongst alcoholic drinks for the hopeless. The last months had been like a trip on the Night Train. Then, thankfully, she felt a surge of anger flushing her whole body. She wasn't going to cry.

'Don't you want this play to be a success?' she said. 'Do you actually enjoy screwing up? Why can't you get behind the words you write? What are you scared of?'

'You don't understand anything,' said the writer. 'You're so very American, Alice. Being American is like having a piece missing in your brain.'

'Oh, yeah,' she said. 'Called irony, right?'

'That's part of it.'

'And being English, that means you'd rather screw up and have people be sorry for you than have expectations of you, right?'

'How very perceptive,' said the writer.

'You asshole,' said Alice.'

The writer rose. It took a little while, and he had to hold is head with one hand and the table with the other, but there he was. Standing up. Through the crook of his elbow she could see the Frenchman looking over.

'Listen,' said Kevin. 'Would you like to know why I chose you, out of all the women in New York?'

'Surprise me.'

'Because you had the first desk on the left. You were nearest, Alice.'

And the writer walked through the revolving doors toward his first drink of the day, leaving the assistant production manager, not for the first time, but perhaps for the last, to pick up the check. Alice was surprised by a sudden flood of relief and elation as she realised that the rest of the day was hers. And she had a good product in her purse for Grant Green.

As she stood at the counter, the Frenchman, as she had known he would, spoke to her.

'Your friend has gone away?'

'Yes, he's gone.'

'You live in New York?'

'Yes, I do.'

'I am French.'

'Yes, I know.'

'Perhaps you could show me the city.'

She looked at him. Close up, his smile was even more

brilliant. Yes, he was certainly lovely, dark and deep, but Alice had promises to keep, and miles to go before she had her own production team. And Kevin Crowe had been a learning experience: what's a learning experience if you don't learn something from it?

'No,' she said. 'I'm sure you're very nice, but I don't need a French baby.'

Moving the
Tables

Neat people, neat people. Characters in a story. They think they know what's happening in their heads, even poor brain-rot Kevin, but it was never like that, Rust knows. And Alice, whose real name (Rust thinks) was Annie, was far more wispy and diffuse, far from being a swinger of birches, much more of a misty shimmerer herself, clicking upon herself in a rising breeze, turning many-coloured as the stir cracked and crazed her fragile crust of recently-acquired Manhattan enamel . . . for example, she owned a big crazy dog called Captain, who brought great anxieties into her life. Passionately jealous of all her other relationships, he would behave in the most extravagant way, on one occasion hurling himself off a quay sixty feet down into the Hudson River because . . . There Rust goes again. How does he know why Annie's dog did that? He doesn't know why anybody does anything, he's just the writer. But he does know this: Alice would never have owned a dog like that, or had such a stormy, passionate relationship with anyone or anything. Though real Annie, like cardboard Alice, was very good at her job and, so far as Rust could understand, ambitious. And she did have the first desk on the left as you went in.

Real. Cardboard. They all turn into cardboard once Rust starts thinking about them.

There wasn't any Grant Green. There were two women producers; a short roundy one who wore blokeish blue pinstripe suits, and had an endearingly donnish manner, rather as if C. S. Lewis had gone into show business; and a tall blonde one who frightened the shit out of everyone, especially Rust. He never felt he got to know them awfully well, and after the play opened he no longer had the chance to get to know anyone.

Rust was so nervous on the press night that he left the theatre at the end of the first act, walked a couple of blocks to his cheap hotel on West 46th St, and spent the second act sitting on the toilet watching Billy Graham on the growling, flickering, ghost-haunted TV set through the half-open bathroom door. The bed was unmade, though the card saying 'Please Make up the Room' had been hanging outside the door all day. On the mottled carpet Rust could see a swiss cheese and coleslaw sandwich which someone, probably Rust himself, had trodden in.

The second act ran sixty-four minutes and ten seconds excluding laughter and applause. Rust pulled his pants up and zapped Billy Graham after sixty-one minutes on the toilet, which gave him just about enough time to get round to the stage door and kiss people. He must have done this, though he doesn't remember a thing about it. He remembers Billy Graham very clearly, though. And he remembers the swiss cheese sandwich.

There was some sort of confusion and discord afterwards about where everyone was going, or maybe they were trying to conceal the true location of the party from the writer. It didn't matter because Rust would have gone to Sardi's even if he had been the only man left in the universe. Rust wanted his shot at Sardi's – it might be the only one he would ever get. (Was, too, as it turned out.) Actually the restaurant did seem strangely diffident in a cruel sort of way, as if paying its respects to a deceased person that nobody privately gave a shit about. There was Rust, and Rust's girlfriend (the one before the German one who broke his heart) and Rust's sweet pink-faced agent Stephen, and a big man from the William Morris agency who looked as if he knew more than he was telling. Over on the far side of the room sat the actor Rust had assumed was gay, with his wife and ten children, all of them mugging away bravely as if they had nothing to hide and nothing to fear, and somehow conveying the exact opposite of this.

The man from the William Morris agency looked up from a careful reading of the menu and announced that he could recommend nothing whatsoever, but everyone managed to order something, and even eat part of it, because there was nothing else to do until the first edition papers arrived. The man from the William Morris agency did all the talking, even supplying the laughs for his own jokes. He seemed to be in league with the waiters in some way, and it was only the next day that Rust realised what their common understanding was.

Then the maitre d' came over with his armful of damp heavy newsprint, flopping a series of piles of it on to the pink table-cloths. Everybody read the reviews, and the silence deepened and intensified until it seemed probable that no one in the company would ever speak again. The essential message of the reviews was that while it was always a pleasure to welcome the great actress back to these shores, it was a shame that she had chosen to manifest herself in this heap of garbage by this hitherto (and doubtless subsequently) unknown English asshole Rust. That was the essential message, but New York critics are not given to brevity and pithiness: all three of them went on to develop this view at length and in detail . . . after a while Rust heard a faint whimpering sound and realised that it was coming from his own throat. He was damp and clammy, and faintly surprised to find that he was not bleeding from every orifice. He looked up and saw that the man from the William Morris agency was grinning. So were the waiters. Though no one had asked them to, the waiters came over then and started to clear the tables.

After that, Rust remembers only fragments of that night. There was a party they gatecrashed in the Ansonia, where Tony Harrison was kind to him and solaced Rust and his girlfriend with bottles of Newcastle Brown and Guinness, and after that again the dark paranoia bars that seemed to crackle like static with the malice of the New York night, then the dive into oblivion, knowing that when he woke up the papers would still be there, part of the dismal pattern, woven into the fabric like the swiss cheese sandwich.

But even then, with no one looking straight at him, he didn't realise that it was he who smelt wrong, and when the great actress phoned him in the morning and invited him for drinks in the Oak Bar in the Plaza it seemed as if things might even then turn out to be all right . . .

And so it was that Rust and his girlfriend sat at the Oak Bar in the Plaza, drooping over steak sandwiches and Bloody Marys, watching the men taking the tables away. That was what was going on in the Oak Bar of the Plaza that day: they were moving the tables. Rust couldn't see where they were taking them from or where they were taking them to. It was just that they seemed to have to take them all through the Oak Bar where Rust was drinking, holding his right hand firmly to the nape of his neck as he lifted the glass to his lips.

The way they moved the tables was like this: they took the legs through first. There were about ten or a dozen men, all carrying these square black table legs through the Oak Bar in a long line, looking neither to the right nor to the left. There must have been a lot of those legs. They were very ordinary, square-sectioned black table legs. Rust could not take his eyes off them. He felt that if he took his eyes off them, the whole operation would founder. He felt part of it, and he felt proud and comforted to be part of it. It was something to do with how many table legs there were, and the sense of dedication and purpose in the hotel employees who were carrying them that was so impressive.

Then they brought the table tops through. These big round table tops. The way they did it: they stood them on their sides and they *rolled* them through the Oak Bar where Rust and Rust's girlfriend and the great actress and the great actress's agent were sitting talking about great European cheeses and silently trying to work out who was to blame.

The great actress's agent told a story about a breed of Swiss dog which had been developed specially to guard cheese in the foothills of the Alps. It was not a bad story, and he drew it out and made it last a good long time. Then a man in a smart suit came over from another table and asked the great actress for her autograph and she smiled very graciously and signed his programme from the night before, and then she told him he should really get Rust's autograph, because Rust had written the play, and he took that very well, and handed the programme to Rust, and Rust signed it, but he could tell that the man didn't like it very much. Rust could see this man as the years went by, saying, 'Look where the great actress signed her name for me!' and seeing them wondering who the other schmuck might be.

Rust thinks that it was round about then that he realised who was to blame.

The men were coming through with these table tops all this time, just rolling them through. They were big and heavy and black and they must have been easily six feet in diameter, because you couldn't see the men rolling them, you could just see their fingers clasping over the edges of the table tops, as if they were hanging on for their lives to the edge of a cliff.

They seemed pretty cheerful about it all though.

There must have been about thirty of these tables altogether.

Rust never wrote a story about this, but when he thinks about that time in New York, that's what he really remembers. Sitting in the Oak Bar the day after the opening, watching the men moving the tables.

Working Well

'Who's that in your bed, Mammy?'

She raised herself on one elbow and saw Alistair's shadowed face, lower lip already out like a shelf, plump hands white and twisting. It was going to be so important to say the right thing now.

'It's all right, Alistair,' she said. 'Everything's all right. You go back to your own nice bed.'

'I want to come in.'

She felt the man shift beside her.

'You can't come in now,' she said. 'Come on, Alistair, you're a big boy now.'

'Can't you get rid of him?' mumbled the man.

'Make him go away, Mammy.'

'I can't make him go away, Alistair. He's your daddy. It's his bed, too.'

'He's not my daddy, make him go away.'

It was so hard to do it right.

'You know he is, Alistair. Don't you? He's your daddy and it's his bed too, and he'll always be sleeping here now, and you've got a nice big boy's bed of your own.'

The plump hands pulling and twisting at the Fair Isle jumper. 'Mammy, let me in!'

Fascinated she watched the plump face crease and quiver; tears, real tears, rolled down the cheeks.

'Mammy, *please*.' High, quavery, hopeless.

She held her breath, waited, and Alistair sank to his knees and sobbed, hands pulling at his hair and face, head bumping over and over again on the carpet.

She had done it right, and she felt horrid. She was alarmed by the strength of her yearning to reach for Alistair, draw him in, soothe and warm him with her softnesses, postpone the pain of his growing for just one more day; but even as she felt it, she had to suppress an even more powerful urge to snort and giggle – worse, let out huge vulgar Tonypandy yelps of laughter at poor Alistair sobbing there on the carpet with his helpless fingers tugging at the Fair Isle jumper rumpled over his fifty-year-old paunch. Big soft dab.

The man beside her, a bearded probation officer she had met for the first time the previous evening, said in a very fair shot at a whiskery Tyneside accent, 'Now that's enough, lad. Go back to bed when your mammy tells you, or you'll feel the back of me hand!'

'I won't.'

'You bloody will!'

'You go now,' said Ellie, 'and Daddy'll give you a game of football right after breakfast, won't you?'

'Aye, if he's a good boy.'

It was as if Alistair hadn't heard. Hugging his round belly, he toppled over sideways and rolled on his back, sucking in great gulps of air and releasing them in rich sonorous tenor sobs and howls. Alistair was working well.

The probation officer heaved himself up and contemplated Alistair with kindly disinterest.

'Aye,' he said gruffly. 'You've turned him into a crybaby between the pair of you.'

He seemed quite pleased about it really. So did Alistair, whose sobs had now taken on a steady rhythmic pattern counterpointed by the drumming of his fat little fists on the carpet. Just as Ellie was beginning to think how easy another person's misery was to take, when you got into the swing of it, so to speak, she heard her own voice, embarrassingly shrill and Welsh.

'Oh, for God's sake, Alistair, shut up, you big baby. You want everything, don't you, you want the whole bloody world and you can't have it, you're not a baby any more! Alistair, if you could just see how *stupid* you look . . .'

She trailed off, feeling her face go hot.

'Sorry,' she said.

Alistair's sobs subsided. He knelt up, reached into his

trouser pocket, and took out his spectacle case. Taking his time, he wiped his eyes and his hornrims with the same bit of cloth, put them on, and stared round at the ring of faces with the air of a man who has done his level best.

'What's going on, Alistair?' asked Kurt quietly.

Alistair put one finger inside his stiff dog-collar. 'I'm not sure, Kurt.'

'Can you stay with the feeling, Alistair?'

'I think it's going now,' said Alistair. 'Yes, I think it's over now. Thank you. Thank you all very much.'

'I think we are all very moved here,' said Kurt. 'You know, there's a whole generation of men walking around who have to deal with the trauma of being expelled from their mothers' beds by fathers returning from the war.'

Alistair looked as if he wasn't too sure whether to be pleased about that or not.

'But that doesn't make it any easier for Alistair,' said the probation officer, reverting to his usual role of Caring Person. Alistair beamed at him.

'Thank you, Sid,' he said. And then, to Ellie's alarm, Alistair crawled straight towards her, and clutched both her hands in his, his plump face dazzlingly close.

'Thank you, Ellie,' he said. 'I couldn't have done that in a million years without you. I haven't wept like that since I was ten years old.'

'Oh, that's OK,' she said nervously. 'You know – any little thing.' Her giggle was like a knife scraping a plate and God, she was blushing *again*. She was going to kill Cy Warner for getting her into this.

'What's going on, Ellie?'

'I don't know. Nothing!' Knowing they could all hear the panic in her voice.

'Who, me sir? Not me sir! No, I never sir!' He was too blinking clever by a long way, this Kurt Ebhart, with his expensive foreign accent and his sly, I-could-be-up-you-like-a-rat-up-a-drain smile. The great thing about Kurt (Cy Warner had told her in what seemed to be the standard discourse for young dons in provincial universities) was that he cut right through all the shit, and when Ellie had replied that she could get all she wanted of that sort of thing with the kittens' dirt tray, Cy had smiled indulgently, and explained that Kurt could see right through the façade to the real person underneath (which Ellie had known perfectly well was what he meant all the time) and that Ellie with her tremendous freshness and honesty and her built-in shit detector (quick flash of kitten turds again) would respond to Kurt very deeply, he was sure.

The trouble at this very moment, though, was that Kurt seemed to be seeing not only through her façade, such as it was, but more particularly through her shirt, worn without a bra as a concession to Alternative Life Strategies; and, though this seemed impossible, through her new jeans, and, not to put too fine a point on it, her knickers.

'Do you have something you'd like to share with the group, Ellie?' (*What did he mean?*)

'What?'

'Do you have something you'd like to work on?'

'Oh. No! I mean, no, no. I'm fine. I'm dying for a cup of tea though. Does anyone else fancy a cup of tea?' No one answered. The group seemed to have re-formed, beaming its interest in on her. She had become the centre of the circle. It looked very much as if it was Get Ellie time. For a moment she felt faint, but she fought it down and stood up.

'Well, I'm going to make some, anyway, all right?' And she stumbled past them out to the kitchen of Kurt's cottage, shut the door behind her, leant on the huge old chipped porcelain sink, and breathed deeply letting her body cool as she stared out through the tiny four-paned window across Swaledale. Two grouse sat on the dry stone wall fifty feet below her. 'Go back,' they said. 'Go back.' But that was what grouse always said, and Ellie was very proud of herself for being here, despite the bad moments. She was not loading the washing machine, she was not ferrying the kids to the swimming pool, she was not, thank God, watching old Graham pounding red-faced all over a squash court, and she was not even trying to get together a bit of deathless prose for sarcastic Cy.

She was doing something for herself, she thought, as she filled the kettle, lit the stove, and began to wash the dozen or so dirty mugs that stood on the draining board. She had hammered up the A1 through shuddering cliffs of container lorries, she had negotiated the hairpin bends from Richmond to Reeth, alone and unaided she had found the cottage from Kurt's eccentric map, and stood blinking in a room full of strangers, assorted bodies and faces with nothing but Christian names to identify them, and herself just herself, just Ellie. A situation of infinite possibilities: a Weekend Encounter Group.

Kurt had explained some of this early on the Friday evening. Sitting cross-legged on his red cushion, his voice perhaps deliberately soft so that his listeners unconsciously stopped fidgeting and leaned towards him, he had suggested that they might regard the weekend as an experiment in alternative living, an opportunity to explore the possibilities within themselves, to see what they could be, without the familiar baggage of their everyday lives (smiling here at a lady called Joan whose three suitcases half filled one of the bedrooms and who had already changed twice since her arrival). To take a mundane example, said Kurt, they would share the food that they had brought and the preparation of it. And they might give themselves permission to waive some of the conventions of the world outside. At this point Sid the probation officer had suggested that an example might be helpful.

'We might consider the bathroom,' said Kurt. 'There is one bathroom, here we are twelve people. It would be convenient, it would save time, it might be a learning experience, it would certainly assist poor Kurt with his heating bills, if we could allow ourselves to leave the door unlocked. The bath is a big one, it has room for two ... it has on occasions accommodated three and even four ...'

Sid, and two or three others who seemed to be old hands, had chuckled benignly at this, and Ellie had felt the panic rise. Kurt had looked straight at her, smiling gently.

'It isn't compulsory, you know. We give ourselves permission to say no as well as yes, if no is right for us. But if something is for us a very big risk, then perhaps our need to take that risk is very big as well.'

Hum, hum, Ellie thought. There was something in this that reminded her of the line of reasoning taken by a fellow member of her local youth club, whose stubbornly self-righteous cock had been pressed upon her attention every Wednesday night during the autumn of her fifteenth year.

But after this threatening introduction, the Friday night had been a doddle, a sort of cross between a children's birthday party and one of Cy Warner's seminars. And as they had shouted, learnt the rules of new games like Psychodrama and Robot, swapped dreams and fantasies, seen each other as animals and articles of furniture (Sid had been kind enough to see Ellie as a chaise-longue) Ellie had discovered that these strangers found her both nice and interesting, something she was going to have to impress on old Graham somehow when she got back.

The next morning, therefore, having crawled out of her son's sleeping-bag, she had bravely left the bathroom door unlocked and sat for a full fifteen minutes in Kurt's big bath, trying her level best not to cross her arms over her breasts as her new friends came in and out on various innocuous errands to do with teeth and gargling. No one offered to get in with her, and she was surprised to find herself mildly disappointed at this.

Then a small, scruffy man called John, who had barely spoken on Friday evening, marched in, dropped his jeans, and sat grimly intent on the lavatory. After five minutes or so of tense silence, he groaned, rose abruptly and pulled his jeans up again, glowering at Ellie.

'You're inhibiting me.'

'Sorry.'

'I've been working on my inhibitions for four fucking years, and now I can't even take a crap in company.'

'Sorry.'

'Well, that's my day ruined.'

This had seemed hardly fair, and she had been about to give him a piece of her mind when he strode out without another word. And that had set the pattern for Saturday. Having spent Friday evening learning how warm and caring they could be together, the group were now, as Kurt put it, exploring the interpersonal tensions and giving themselves permission to be honest with themselves and each other. Giving themselves permission to show off and be nasty was more like it, Ellie thought.

There was a pattern to it all that she was beginning to recognise. Someone would say something that attracted attention, and would then be badgered by the group into *exploring their feelings*. This might result in a shouting match, a wrestling match, or more usually, in the impromptu dramatisation of some unpleasant memory. This in turn would lead to a healthy release of emotion, climaxing with a good old cry and a noisy session of beating hell out of a cushion until the beater was exhausted. (From the sounds in the other room, it seemed that Alistair might have reached the climax now.)

After this, the other members of the group would soothe, cuddle, caress, massage and generally muck about with him, and if all went well this orgy of tenderness would make some other poor dab burst into tears. Kurt would ask the other poor dab what was going on, and the whole cycle would start again.

It did not seem the moment to take the tea in, as several people besides Alistair sounded as if they were sobbing now. She looked out of the window again. The grouse, having taken their own advice perhaps, had gone. The bare wall looked peculiarly close and clear as if the air had acquired some extra transparency. She could see individual blades of grass bending in the wind. She looked down at her hand: freckles, creases, downy hair, and suddenly felt absurdly fond of it, grateful that it had come all this way with her. Nice hand. Things, she felt, could definitely be all right.

The door opened and John came in.
    'Need any help?'
    'You time things just like my husband does. It's all ready.'
    'Ah.'
    He picked up a mug and drank from it.
    'Good tea,' he said.
    'Well, I've had the practice, haven't I?' Letting the Tony-pandy come out on purpose this time.

'You don't need all that shit.'

'Oh. Thank you.'

'Or that shit,' he added, jerking his head towards the group-groan from the other room.

'But it's . . . well, it's important for Alistair, isn't it? – He seemed to be going through something very important there . . .'

'He's dragged that mammy's bed of his round every group in the country. I don't know how many times I've seen it now. He just gets off on it. Lobstein's pissed off with it. Lobstein won't have him any more. Lobstein kicked him out. You been to Lobstein's groups?'

'No, this is my first one.'

'You want to try Lobstein. He *really* cuts through the shit.'

Ellie was not exactly sure how it came about that at ten o'clock that evening she was shuffling slowly round a darkened room, naked, with her eyes shut, and in the company of eleven other naked people similarly occupied. It was a very odd feeling. Things changed so rapidly: at one moment the room seemed impossibly full of bodies at the next she felt that everyone had gone away somewhere, that she was wondering alone in a huge lonely space. Kurt's voice was almost a whisper. Where was it coming from?

'Touch, and pass on. Anything you feel is all right. Doesn't matter who it is. Acknowledge, and pass on.'

The panic buzzing in her ears had stopped now, and her fingers were not trembling any more. What does it matter, Ellie, nobody knows you here.' she said to herself, and was able for the first time to notice things outside herself, the extraordinary disparity of people's sizes and shapes; how hard and stiff the men were, how rounded and yielding even the thinnest of the women. A new thing, this. Was this how she felt to old Graham? No wonder they like us so much, she thought. She let her hands fall to her sides and moved more slowly, letting her shy, companionable body make its own discoveries.

There was some sort of impasse in front of her, she could tell, sensitive enough to feel the warmth of breath, the humanly filled air, before she touched an obstacle. Yes, several people seemed to have come to a halt. She turned to the right, a little off balance, and found herself leaning against someone a little shorter than herself, whose skin smelled sharply sweet, like haylofts. A hand touched her shoulder reassuringly and she snuggled for a moment. Nice. Short hair. It must be – what was her name? – Darlene. A moment later she realised that it was hardly likely that Darlene would be sporting such a surprisingly long flaccid penis. It seemed as natural to take it in her hand as to take a toddler's hand to cross the road. Well, fancy that. Kurt Ebhart had been right: everything *was* possible.

'OK.' It was almost a whisper. 'Draw together in the centre. Let yourself be drawn in.'

Unobstrusively relinquishing Darlene's penis as she realised that Kurt had probably had his eyes open all the time, Ellie let herself be drawn in.

'If you are on the outside, see how many people you can enclose. If you are on the inside, just let it happen.' Ellie was on the inside and she let it happen: a qualitative intensification of darkness, a mingling of body smells, her nose jammed into a hairy chest. Graham would be watching *Match of The Day*, Erin would be on her way back from the tin hut disco . . . she was sinking down. The weight of the circle was pressing on her. Someone was collapsing the Group. Four Die in Body Spillage.

'Relax,' said Kurt Ebhart. 'Let it happen.'

She was awake and it was dawn. Carefully she eased herself apart from the Ebhart body. The care was superfluous: he lay still as death beside her. Well, so that had happened, she had not dreamed it, and she had been right about him. When, in the darkness of the living room she had felt a practised and determined hand exploring parts of her she still liked to feel were in some way private, she had opened her eyes, and that had, as it were, blown it as far as relaxing and letting it happen were concerned. What had seemed an orgy of pure friendliness with knobs on, so to speak, was becoming all too obviously an anxious, fumbling affair, the indiscriminate hunger of a bunch of very lonely people, and she had wriggled out of the warm sweaty heap and crept upstairs to her sleeping bag and slipped into a deep and dreamless sleep.

She wasn't quite sure at what moment her zip had been drawn down and Kurt had slid his long bony body in beside her, and she had been too sleepy to take in much of what he had said, but after he had mumbled for a long while about his disappointments and his weakness and his needs and, finally, his vasectomy, she had shyly and companionably invited him to enter her, which he had accomplished with some little difficulty. When she felt him quicken, she said, 'Come on, then,' which made her giggle aloud, because that was what she said to Graham too, and the kittens at bedtime, come to that, and he had come, like the kittens, with a little whimpering mew.

She wriggled upwards until she was free of the sleeping bag, pulled on her shirt, and tiptoed downstairs. Outside it was cold, a hint of frost on Kurt's wizened sheep-nibbled rosebushes. Far down in the valley someone was trying to start a van. Soon she would have to start her little car and take her insights home with her. But what had she done there, what had she got? She had played the games well, she had made them tea, she had kept them away from her private parts. Bare feet on the cold stone, dawn breeze playing around her legs, she felt like . . . she felt like herself. She could, perhaps, take that back with her.

Suddenly she heard a crashing sound in the grass, close and loud enough to be alarming. She turned and saw a hedgehog family, a mother, she supposed, and four little ones trundling in a noisy convoy through the tussocks.

'Hey,' she said. 'Come here.'

They took no notice of her, neither quickening nor slowing their pace, making no effort to hide. They had no fear. What was it Cy had said? 'The fox knows many things, but the hedgehog knows one big thing.'

She watched them out of sight, turned, and went back into the house.

Roger was working now. He had told them a long and tearful rigmarole about how he never got what he wanted in life, instancing the occasion when he and some friends had got together this acid trip, right, and how typical this was of the way his so-called friends bloody treated him, the idea being that they were supposed to be looking after him, right, and giving him a really nice trip, but the way it finished up was that two of them had only gone and left him, right, only just got up and walked out on him, and he, Roger, had finished up looking after this other guy he didn't even know, and the way it had turned out was that this other guy had taken the acid and had the trip while Roger had to stay with him and see him through it and bring him down, when it was supposed to be Roger's trip, right, and he never even liked this guy anyway, and that was an example of how he never got what he bloody wanted.

'Go round the group,' said Kurt. 'Take a risk. Ask each of them for something. Ask each of them for their love and attention.'

Roger went round the group, and even Ellie could see how clearly he alienated everyone with his tears and his self-pity and his petulance, and how if they hadn't all been on their best behaviour and writing him emotional cheques they'd never have to honour, in real life they would get up and walk away from him just as his acid freak friends had done.

So when it came to her turn, she said, 'You could be all right, Roger, but the way you are now, you're just a pain. You want everyone's love and attention but you don't want to give anything back. Only babies can get away with that. You're just a big baby that nobody wants.'

After a pause, Kurt said quietly, 'Ellie, you're full of shit, aren't you?'

She couldn't believe her ears.

'I was only trying to be honest, I thought that was what we were supposed to do. I'm sorry if I – '

'You're full of shit, Ellie. Everybody's a baby and you're the only grown-up in the room, right?'

'No, I didn't mean that.'

'That's what I hear from you. That's what Alistair heard from you. Now Roger. What's all this shit about babies, Ellie?'

'I don't know. I've had babies, I s'pose, I know how they go on.'

'Shit.'

She was red again. 'Do you mind not saying that all the time?'

'Ellie, would you do something for me?'

'What?'

'Would you try saying to the group: "I'm a baby. I want your love and affection and I won't give you anything back. I'm a baby and no one loves me."'

'No, I won't,' she said.

'Why not, Ellie?'

'Because it's so stupid! I don't think that at all. I mean, there people here who really need help with problems, it's a waste of everyone's time . . .'

'Just to please us, Ellie. If it's stupid it won't take long, and it won't hurt, and then we'll get off your back and you can go home to your nice house and your nice husband.'

She felt the hungry lonely eyes on her. Alistair. John. Joan. Darlene. Roger. Sid. Her friends and fellow-sufferers. She could play this game for them.

'I'm a baby,' she said. 'I want your love and affection and I won't give you a thing. I'm a baby . . . and no one loves me.' She felt fine. It was just her voice that was odd, something thick in her throat.

'Again.'

'I'm a baby. I want your love and affection and I . . .' and then she was crying – it was so strange – and her voice went up and down, and she tried to finish the sentence but the words had gone bubbling off in her chest somewhere, and she couldn't seem to get her breath.

'OK' said Kurt very quietly. 'Fine.'

Through her tears she could see the circle of bright faces, and they were smiling, they were smiling at her fondly.

Ellie was working well.

Moose
Bulletin

MEMORANDUM NO. 7

From: 'Uncle Stephen'
To: All my Nephews and Nieces
Subject: Trojan Moose

1. Accreditation

Please treat 'Uncle Stephen' with the respect you would normally accord to, er, someone very important in the organisation. As several new data virus varieties appear to have been triggered by the appearance on a document of the names, job titles, or job descriptions of 'great big clever blokes like Uncle Stephen' we have been forced to adopt the above nomenclature.

1. The problem

'The Moose' as it has come to be known was first sighted in the Social Studies faculty at the University of Warwick. The Moose is a sophisticated data virus of the Trojan Horse variety. The Moose destroys data at a rate of knots. Do not be fooled by The Moose. The Moose looks user-friendly but he is a killer.

2. What triggers The Moose?

A lot of things seem to get The Moose going. Here are some of them:

(more)

Articles with footnotes, especially if the footnotes contain the word 'ibid'.

The phrases 'unpack this metaphor' and 'unpack this problem'. In fact, any use of the word 'unpack' except when applied to luggage appears to provoke The Moose to rip data to shreds.

Words like 'resonate' or 'accountability'.

Any reference to knowing where someone or something is coming from, except in the strict geographical sense.

Unfortunately it is not possible to be more precise at the moment but detailed research is in progress. However it can be immediately grasped from the examples above that Social Studies faculties will be exceptionally vulnerable to Moose attack.

3. What is a Moose attack like?

Typically the Moose will appear to loom up from the bottom of the screen towards the end of a lengthy document. He will appear as a line drawing of the head and shoulders of a mature male moose with a full set of antlers. He will have a cartoon bubble issuing from his mouth saying, 'Hi there! It's the Moose!'

There is no further warning. What happens next is that all the letters and digits in the article 'float' downwards rather like snowflakes, and appear to lie in a jumbled heap at the bottom of the screen.

The Moose frequently hits the same target twice. Typically he will wait until the systems user has laboriously reconstructed his document and is nearly at the end of it. On his second appearance the Moose will often be seen to appear upside down at the top of the screen, with a bubble saying, 'Hi there! The Moose is

(more)

back!' The letters and digits will immediately float upwards and gather in a kind of encrustation or frosting along the top edge of the screen.

4. Techniques for recovering data lost through Moose attack

There are no techniques for recovering data lost through Moose attack. You simply have to start again from the beginning, with no guarantee that the Moose will not hit you again and again.

5. Precautions to take against Moose attack

If the Moose is into your nerve centre, there is nothing you can do. If your system is so far Moose-free, it helps to avoid all casually-acquired software, particularly games. But Moose have been known to lie dormant within information systems for as long as seven years.

6. Moose Attacks on the Human Brain

Recently there have been several reports of Moose attacks on the human brain. These are sometimes preceded by dreams about moose. Moose attacks on the brain, or mooserot attacks as they are sometimes known, are very similar to moose attacks on minis and mainframes. The human brain is of course, amongst other things, a device for storage retrieval and restructuring of data. The Moose simply invades these structures and deconstructs them.

7. How will I know whether I am harbouring a Moose?

There is no way of knowing until the Moose makes himself known. But you may find that nothing makes sense any more and your friends treat you differently. You may suddenly lose your job, or be attacked by groups of strangers. But all these things also happen to people who are not subject to Moose invasion.

(more)

8. How can I be sure that the Moose has not colonised this very memorandum?

Don't you understand *anything*? Of *course* you can't be sure of that, or anything else for that matter. Stop asking these silly questions. We have important work to do here.

(ends)

The Worst Thing

– anybody ever said to you, I mean. Like when they said it, you thought, yes, that's the worst thing I ever heard, that's the worst thing they could have said to me just then.

– Yes, I do have a purpose in asking you that; you know me, nothing's ever just idle curiosity with me . . . now I come to think of it, I doubt whether it is with anybody, ever – it's never *just* idle curiosity, is it? We are all curious about each other, I know. More curious about some than others, though, right?

– What do I mean? Like you always seemed to be curious about us, about me and Carole, and we, well, me at any rate, I've always been interested in you, ever since I first met you. Sort of attraction of opposites. You being a writer. Me being, well . . . someone who had always done physical work, always worked with my hands. Plastering. Boxing. Bouncing, a bit. Always seem to have to operate in . . . in the more colourful segment of the manual work spectrum. Always something a bit flash, a bit magical. Pablo Picasso, right? If Pablo Picasso had gone in for the building trade, he'd have been a plasterer, flash git as he was. Quick hands. Like me. I could have been a painter. Still could. I'm talking about fine art, not painting and decorating. Why not? I was fucking brilliant at art in school. Well, you've seen some of my pictures. It's all right, I won't ask you what you think of them.

– No, you don't understand. I don't *want* to know, they're for me, not for you, I don't fucking well care what you think of them, right? No offence. Cheers. But . . . I often think what it might be like to be a full-time artist. Get up . . . come downstairs . . . do some painting . . . go down the pub . . . come back . . . have a look at it . . . do some more . . . go to bed. Then, next day, same thing . . . I'd like that. I think that would be a very pure life. Like, independent. Free. *Pure*.

– The thing about you: you don't lead a pure life. No, hang on. You do your writing, but you depend on people like me and Carole. Raw material, right? That's the sort of writer you are. Don't take this wrong, but you're parasitical on us, aren't you? We . . . enjoy . . . a symbiotic relationship. The other side of which is: by choosing our lives to write about, you're like – how shall I put it? – conferring dignity and significance on our lives. Or patronising our bollocks off – I've never been quite sure.

– No, listen. You put yourself about a bit in your stories and plays and that, but you always wonder what it must be like to put yourself about a bit in real life, don't you? Just like I wonder what it must be like to make up all those stories. And Carole, going to that writing class of yours. What do you think of her stories, by the way?

– That a fact? No, you're being too kind, Andy. Come on. They're crap, really, aren't they? She's never been able to make anything up, Carole. Couldn't tell a lie to save her life. Well, she tries, but no way does she succeed. Same with me. I'd love to make up stories, but the only stories I can tell are true ones. And they can get you into trouble too, am I right? Been there, have we? Had time to think now? About the worst thing?

– It's funny, I've come to think of you as a, as a really close friend, even though we haven't known each other that long . . . like we have a rapport going; sometimes, even, one of us can tell what the other one is thinking, when we've had a few especially. I sort of love those, those slow clairvoyant thought patterns . . . and we have had a few today of course, a bit of steady, sensible, slow afternoon drinking. We have put away a few. We're not ratted. We're not arseholed. Far from it. We're just right. But we're not clairvoyant. We're not ready for the Zen darts. We're not tuned to the same wavelength. Maybe it's just one of those days when I look at you and think, what is this smug fuck doing in my life, is he just amusing himself at my expense, is he just – what's that word? – *slumming*? And no, since you don't ask, Carole never feels like that, she says she's never felt patronised by you, she says she's never seen you as a . . . tourist.

– Anyway, this time I was thinking of, I was down the club, the Edwardian, where we were last Sunday, yeah? The second place. With all the potted palms? And that huge big painting of Lady Godiva, all very tasteful and pre-Raphaelite; I know the bloke who does those, yeah, cheers, right, quite chic for downtown Cov. Well they'd closed it for a private function, but I'd been invited to stick around, nobody had told me what my, like, status was, whether I was a guest or on the staff, or what, that evening. Denny Grieve was on the door, and he's very useful, a very sought-after man for functions . . . anyway, it was a private party. Very quiet. No one was about to get stroppy. The thing was, John Ward and his brother had come up from London. John *Ward*. The *Wards*. You never heard of them? Well, if you've never heard of them, that . . . oh, never mind. Let's say some very heavy people had come up from London, three carloads of them. And they were having a little function in the Edwardian that was partly social and mostly business. And I'd been told to stick around but I didn't know what my status was. After about a couple of hours, it settled down to some serious talking, and I was very definitely not invited in on that. I recognised a couple of the local bookies and a dodgy barrister from Nottingham.

– Well, I didn't fancy talking to John Ward's foot soldiers, you know me, I like an intelligent conversation, I like to talk about the meaning of life. Like the talks *we* have. Yes, all right. Yes, I will. Cheers. They'd brought a couple of tarts down with them. One of them sat at the table with the foot soldiers, and the other one was sat at the bar on a stool, where I was sitting. Not right next to me. There were, like, two stools between us. And we were both sort of having a drink . . . just sitting there, both of us, not talking to each

other, just looking straight ahead, and drinking our drinks . . .
I'd been drinking all afternoon and it was well on in the
evening by now; I suppose I'd had about ten – I wasn't gone,
but I was comfortable. I don't know if she'd been drinking or
not. And I was getting a bit pissed off with the whole thing,
I was feeling like the spare prick at a wedding. So silly. I had
no idea this was John Ward's wife, no reason why I should
have, but obviously she belonged to him, or to his brother.

– Yeah, yeah, nobody belongs to anybody else, yeah, heard it.
Nobody belongs to anybody else, except they do. Oh, they
do. They do.

– I say, 'looking straight ahead', but there was this big mirror
behind the bar, and if you stare straight ahead all you see is
your own face, and I don't like that, not as a rule. I don't care
to watch myself drinking, so like most people I don't stare
quite straight ahead. I was using the mirror to look round the
room behind me. One big table where the Ward brothers were
doing their serious business. Another big table where the
spare tart was sitting with the foot soldiers. And a few small
tables with people at them: spare pricks. Denny Grieve on
the door, as I said. I was looking at the foot soldiers' table.
They looked pretty much what you would expect, a bunch of
hard-looking blokes in very smart respectable suits. Almost
old-fashioned. The Wards *are* old-fashioned. They're a very
old-established firm. They even operate a colour bar, which
is virtually unknown these days.

– Anyway, as I said, pretty much what you would expect,
except for this one bloke, and he was dressed like the others,
he was just so big and mean-looking. He was huge, really.
About six five or six six. Huge. And nasty-looking with it.
And I had a feeling I'd seen him before, seen him, not met
him. Couldn't think where. I didn't think I'd seen him fight.
And for all he looked so big and hard, I didn't think he was
a fighter. I think it was because every fighter's been beat at
least once, and he didn't look as if he knew what it was to
get beat. I was right about that, as it turned out. He wasn't a
fighter, he was a fucking executioner.

100

– Well, he must have felt me looking at him, because he caught my eye in the mirror, and when I looked away I caught the eye of this tart girl woman who turned out to be John Ward's wife, but I didn't know it then, and she gave me this sort of rueful smile thing, like she was saying what's a couple of sophisticates like you and me doing in this manky old craphole, and we started talking . . . I think I said something about how I'd have to get going soon 'cause I had to take the dog out, and she said what sort of dog, and before we knew where we was we were having this very nice and quite deep conversation about dogs and people and the meaning of life . . . like trust and loyalty . . . what you risk by giving your love to a dog or to a person . . . dogs having such a short life-span . . . and people being such shitty treacherous scumbags. We had a nice little rapport going . . . I was making her laugh a bit, and we were, we were warming to each other. I don't think I'm deluding myself when I say I know I could have been up her like a rat up a drain if I had so wished.

– But I didn't wish to. Neither did she. I could tell that. Neither of us wished to. This wasn't anything to do with being prudent, this wasn't anything to do with her being John Ward's wife; as I say, I didn't even know that then. No, this was partly to do with me belonging to Carole, but mostly to do with the feeling that sometimes it's nice knowing you could, but not. D'you know what I mean, Andy? Have you ever had that feeling? Yeah, once, for about five seconds, right? Joke. Joke.

– But what with the stuff I'd supped and the pleasure of the meaning of life conversation and the rapport with the tart, I'd got myself a bit cut off from the atmosphere in the room at large, and it suddenly got borne in upon me that this atmosphere had sort of . . . thickened. Acquired extra layers of . . . density, somehow. There seemed to be some sort of focus, some sort of triangulation, and it seemed to be concentrated on me; on me and this tart at the bar. It seemed to be down to me to ease it, in some sort of way. So I kind of slid down off the stool and wandered over to one of the empty tables against the wall, and lit a cigarette up and did my level

101

best to look really out of it . . . it just seemed like a bad idea to be focussing on anything or anybody. I had the feeling that I should have kept going, walked right out of the club, but I didn't see any reason for that. After all, it wasn't as if I'd done anything wrong.

– After a couple of minutes I was aware that the very big bloke had got up and was walking over to my table. I didn't make too much of that, I mean it wasn't as if the room had fallen silent, in fact the atmosphere had eased if anything, the Wards had started up their conversation again . . . I suppose I thought he might be coming to ask me to join him at the foot soldiers' table and stop being so bleeding unsociable, something like that. So when he hit me I was really astonished.

– We've talked about violence before, haven't we? You used to get in fights when you were a kid, you know what it's like, hitting people and getting hit. Right? Well, you do and you don't. Because, even though it's all the same thing in one way, in another way it's not. It's all relative, but the relative force of it makes it seem like two completely different things. See – if I was to hit you as hard as I could, you wouldn't just be hurt. You would be amazed and alarmed. You would be astonished that one man could hit another man with such . . . terrible, destructive force. One thing to see it on the telly, quite another thing to experience it for yourself.

– Well, it was like that for me in the Edwardian. I sort of got a glimpse of him swinging . . . and I never quite passed out. He just hit me the once, he caught me on the side of the head. I didn't even realise I was lying on the floor at first, I thought I was still on my feet. When I could see again, I could see him walking back to the big table. No one seemed to have taken much notice. I felt as if I'd been in a road accident or something. I couldn't believe he'd done that with just his fist; I'd never been hit as hard as that in my whole life. There was no question of retaliation. I felt as weak as a baby, and I was starting to worry a bit about my head; it felt actually damaged in there, as if his fist had actually broken my head . . . I remember thinking, I need to get to hospital, get this head looked at. Still had no idea what this was all about. That was the least of my worries.

– After a bit I managed to get up, and I got myself over to Denny Grieve who was still standing by the door. I was feeling a bit giddy and I could see the big man looking over. A few of them were looking over. I asked Denny if he'd seen what happened, and if he had any idea what it was all about. He said, 'Can you walk?' I said yes, I thought I could.

'Well,' he said, 'don't walk – run. Run out to the car park, get in your car, and keep going.'

– Well that sounded like good advice to me. I thought I could drive straight round to the Coventry and Warwickshire casualty ward. It was raining out and I felt cold and shivery, but even though I couldn't run, I managed to walk all right over to the car. I had the key in the lock when I heard these footsteps, and I turned round and there he was, the big fellow, walking quite slowly towards me. And I don't know why, but suddenly I knew that everything was going to be all right, he'd realised it had all been a mistake, and he'd come to apologise, maybe to invite me back in for a drink on John Ward . . . anyway, what he did say was, 'I've come to finish you off.'

Funny how many thoughts can go through your mind in a few seconds – in fact that was what Graham said next, is still in the middle of explaining – but honestly, honestly, all that wind-up just to get to this, talk about the banality of terror, and this such unmodishly, tediously blokeish terror, the fear of being bashed up by someone whose fists are bigger and harder than yours. What about the more subtle, insidious manifestations of fear; the foggy, wavering, damply sooty apparitions of despair, the sickening lurch of sudden identity loss, the cracked disintegrating compass of a wonky sexual orientation . . . yes, I confess, I have used you, Graham, used both you and Carole, sucked off more than one story from your warm and throbbing lives . . . But not this one, honestly, not this lurid melodrama. I can't use this; look, I mean honestly, tart girl, woman wife – the women in this don't even have names for Christ's sake. I mean, I am interested in writing fictions that Jeanette fucking Winterson might want to read, need I say more! Well yes in fairness, yes, I suppose I should, because for you this was not fiction, Graham – that man really did say that to you in that particular car park on that particular night, and I do, I really do understand how dreadful, how finally dreadful it must have been to hear those words, to believe that your young life was about to end, violently, anonymously, and – let's not forget – excruciatingly painfully, on that rain-soaked concrete.

On the other hand, it didn't did it! Because here you are to tell it; which means the story isn't even bloody over yet. I must say I find that very irritating. I don't really want to hear any more about how 'with one bound you were free', or whatever. In fact, and I don't quite know how I'm going to explain this to you, Graham, I don't think I'm going to be able to use you any more. That doesn't go for Carole. Carole's hardness and softnesses, Carole's supple grip on life as we shall be living it in the nineties, Carole's wry wit and occasional rollicking laugh, Carole's dizzingly bright brown eyes . . . well, enough to say that Carole's richnesses are far from being exhausted, and I look forward to exploring Carole in depth and exploiting Carole in all media for quite some time to come.

In the meantime, here's Graham, and it would be churlish to deny him his conclusion, which can't after all be very far away now, can it!

– Police car happened to come by, didn't it? No one had called it or anything. Not that I knew anything about it; apparently he was stamping on my face when they got to him. I was two weeks in hospital and three months off work. I didn't press charges. I'm stupid, but not that stupid. And still none the wiser about what it was all about. Anyway, good as new now, bar the facial scarring and funnily enough this left wrist. Doesn't hurt, just crooked. Lucky. Right?

– Went back to work, we were finishing off this conversion on a big old house in Earlsdon. Looked out of the window, saw this big Jag pull up outside, and four blokes got out, and one of them was the big fellow, the one that had nearly killed me. I wanted to run away, but I couldn't make my legs move. I've never in my life been so frightened. They came in the house and they came upstairs where I was, and they said, 'John Ward wants to have a chat with you, all right?' I couldn't speak to answer them. They had to practically carry me out to the car, my legs were like jelly. They took me to this flash block of flats overlooking the Memorial Park. Right up the top. Not a word spoken all the way. Up in the lift, right up to the top. I thought they were going to throw me off the balcony.

– They take me into the flat . . . it's like a penthouse sort of thing. There's John Ward, sitting behind a big desk. Oh, Graham, he says, good of you to come, appreciate it. I believe I owe you an apology. That bit of unpleasantness was the result of a misunderstanding, I'm very embarrassed. Someone was supposed to have been shafting my wife, and someone pointed you out as that person – mistaken identity, pure and simple. Would two thousand pounds cover it? And he holds out his hand with this big bunch of notes, and I still can't say anything, I just take it, and get out of there, I'm so scared, because I know, those people, they can do just what they like with me.

– Have another drink. No, go on.

– I advise you to. Have another drink.

– I don't know whether I strike you as an easy going person or not, I suppose I am in some ways, but not in others. One thing you might not have appreciated about me is that I am very possessive, I'm a very jealous man. Primitive, I suppose.

– Drink up.

– I don't know whether you have any inkling of what I'm

going to say to you, I hope you have because you don't get the full flavour of it unless you've been anticipating it for a little while.

– You know that phrase, when someone says 'I'm going to beat the shit out of you.' I expect you think of it as a rather corny figure of speech, but it isn't. Not always. Sometimes it's the literal truth.

– All right. Here it comes. And I hope it really is the worst thing anyone ever said to you. You've been messing about with Carole, and now I am going to beat the shit out of you.

Moose Update

MEMORANDUM NO. 8A

From: the Usual Source
To: whom it may concern
Subject: current intelligence on Trojan Moose.

1. We are now able to adopt a relatively bullish stance in relation to, er, infiltration by big chaps with booming voices and antlers. It has not been easy. And there have of course been losses. Which we deeply regret. But we have come through. Recent indications are that the unit is now free from free from free to free two free four five and a half six pence six pence suck you off for sixpence guvnor *oh Christ now* what has somebody hooked up to that contaminated fax or what I mean what is going on here is anybody there isn't it awfully hot in here I feel a bit feel a bit feel a bit cancel erase this memo is contaminated cancel erase I repeat come on big boy gargle my juice I said cancel cancel cancel are you *there*?

> *Moose odour*
> *moose juice*
> *moose smell on the wind.*
> *Ole man moose he comin on down*
> *he go thud thud thud*
> *he battering on your brain*
> *and you don't know whether he on the outside*
> *battering to get in or on the*
> *inside battering to get out*
> *ole man moose on the midnight train*
> *ole man moose takin over yo brain*
> *yes sir.*

I give you a clue I tell you one thing he do,
sometimes he climb right in to the middle of a story
an you don't know which is the right thing
an you don't know which is the middle of the night
thing.

No no no, I said *cancel.*

(ends)

Inappropriate Behaviour

My sister Shirley, she doesn't talk. She's not a baby. She's seventeen years old. She's not deaf and dumb. She's not brain damaged and she's not stupid. She's probably got more brains than you have. She used to talk as much as you or me. See, she *can* talk. But she doesn't talk. You might see her smile, you might see her frown, you might even hear her hum a tune, but she won't talk. Not to anyone. Not a word. Not ever. So that's your first puzzle.

It's all right with me if she don't talk. Shirley's all right. I like Shirley. About the only person I do like, bar one.

Three things I can do: ride, drive, shoot. I can ride any horse you bring me. Teach him his manners. School him, jump him, anything you like. I could teach you to ride a horse, even. Drive any vehicle. Car. Tractor. HGV, even. I could put a Land Rover up a one in two and not roll him. Only trouble is, I haven't got a licence, not old enough, see. And I can shoot a gun.

Here's some things I know that I didn't learn in school: pigs are evil bastards, and they don't pay, not with the new regulations they have now. A milk round, on the other hand, can be a very good living. More farmers blow their brains out than any other kind of person. That's because most farmers have guns. If everyone had guns, they'd all be at it. See that shotgun on the table there. See that other one standing in the corner. And there's another one in the Land Rover. One each, right? No wonder farmers are always shooting themselves. Well, that's some of the things I didn't learn in school.

113

Trouble is, I have to go to school. One of my troubles.

All I asked for was for them to leave us alone, me and Shirl. We could have run this place easy, I could have looked after this place since I was thirteen. And had time for the riding. That's the best. The riding. Not getting dressed up, not the competitions, just it, the thing itself, getting on that big bugger's back, feeling it, all of it, making him feel it, winding him up, and then letting him go. Blaaaaaaaaaagh. Like riding an express train. Like ... I can't explain. You have to do it to know it.

Who would have thought it would have started so bad, the day I met her? The night before, my dad had put his back out again, don't ask me how, so it was me doing the milk round on me own. Up at four, done that, bloody hard work doing a milk round on your own, if you don't believe me, try it ... but I love it coming back, with the sun just getting a little bit warm, all on me own, nobody to get on me nerves, driving the flat up the track, not a soul in sight. I feel happy then, and there is a song I sing, and the name of the song is *Rubber Dolly*. I don't know why I sing that song in particular. I sometimes wonder what that rubber dolly might be like and why she wanted it so much, the little girl in the song.

I can't remember if I was singing it that morning. I got back, had a bit of a wash, and then it was down to that bastard to take me to school, and he was moaning away: bloody kids, bloody holes in your bloody wallet, might as well blow your bloody brains out, and then the Land Rover wouldn't start, hear him then: damn and bugger it, bugger won't buggering start, it's buggered, we'll have to go in the other bugger. The other bugger is the milk float; I hate it when I have to go to school in that, I hate it when kids see me with that sod at all. My father I mean. Listening to kids talk, I think many of them hate and despise their parents, but few with such good reason as I have.

I was late, and they were all in assembly and I could see some of them looking through the windows and pointing at me.

Old Hawke was in the corridor and she gave me a bollocking about being late and improperly dressed, on and on . . . that fat cow never listens to a word you say, so I just turned and walked off while she was still talking and went in the toilets. Valerie Simms and two other girls were in there but I ignored them and went in the cubicle but I could hear them talking about me and my family and about Shirley, anything like that always chokes me up, and I opened the door and came out of that toilet like a bat out of hell, see Valerie Simms' face, scared wasn't in it; I gave her a right seeing to, well I could have done, but about ten people pulled me off of her before I'd hit her more than about three times . . . and that was how I got to meet the new counsellor. Miss McLoughlin. I didn't know what her first name was then, I'd only ever seen her from a distance.

She had this little room, and she'd done it all nice, with flowers on the table and that, and soft chairs, and she asked me to sit down, and she said, 'OK, Helen, I'd like to see if we can talk about some of your behaviours in a non-judgmental way and when we've done that we might look at any ideas you might have about modifying them . . . you might feel on reflection that some of it could be called *inappropriate behaviour.*'

She smiled when she said that, sort of a hospital smile. I thought that first day that she didn't look like anyone who belonged in a school. People who work in our school have operations to take the excitement out of them before they are allowed to start work, and she didn't look as if she had had that operation. I thought she looked a bit like a little girl playing nurses; I don't know why I thought that. It was like she'd learnt this part and she was very excited about playing it. In another way, she looked a bit like something to play with herself. Her hair was all very neat and shiny, all pulled back with a little ribbon, and she had red lipstick on, all very neatly filled in, and this white white blouse with its little collar that looked brand new. But her eyes were not like a doll's eyes, they were quite small and bright and brown and darty, like a rat's eyes, and if you looked close you could see a little bit of downy whiskers on her upper lip. Dark downy whiskers. On her arms as well. Ratty whiskers. I didn't mind that. I thought they suited her.

She was saying that I had got into a rather destructive transactional pattern with the teachers and the other kids at the school which was not helping anyone. She had some of my reports from the junior school about how I was top of the class and popular and everything and she asked if I was happier then. I said I thought that it was bloody obvious I was happier then. She asked me if I would like to break this cycle of confrontations and retaliatory behaviour and I said what I really wanted was to stop going to school altogether, but if they would stop I might. She said, would I like her to negotiate a contract for me? She called it a contract. I would agree to reduce some of my behaviours, like hitting kids who hadn't hit me first, and swearing at the teachers; and they would reduce some of their behaviours, like moaning at me for being late and giving them dumb insolence. I said she could fix it up if she liked, I wasn't listening that hard really, I was looking at her and thinking mad stuff, like it would be nice to take her home and play with her like a Cindy, she looked so nice and clean.

She seemed dead pleased I had said yes about her contract, and in her nice little room it felt for a minute like my life was going to change. But when I got home everything was the same. My mum was up the tree calling the ducks home, and the dogs had eaten our tea, and my sodding dad was still moaning about his back being out. No sign of Shirley. I went upstairs and she was sitting on the bed, I only needed one look at her face. Not all that bad then, his back. That was what I really needed to change my life – him out of it. I gave Shirley a cuddle and went down and rode the horses till it got dark, nothing else to be done.

Next time I went to see Miss McLoughlin she had her contract all drawn up and she'd got the teachers to sign it, even old Hawke. And she said she wanted me to tell her about the things I was good at and the things I liked doing. So I told her about the riding and driving and shooting, like I told you.

And she said, 'Helen, I'm really impressed. I think those are skills anyone would be proud of.' That got me angry when she said that, it was the way she said it, like she didn't really mean it, she had her hospital smile on, and she sounded like one of the Hatton doctors, and I wanted to smash her face in, but I just knocked her vase of flowers on the floor instead. Modifying my behaviour, I suppose. Scared her, though. I was sorry then. Didn't mean to scare her, didn't mean to scare my little Cindy doll.

I said I was sorry and she asked me what it was, what was upsetting me, and I said I couldn't tell her, not in school, and that was true, half true anyway; I was always choking up in school. She said, where then? And then it came to me, what I wanted was to teach her something, she could come to the farm and I could teach her to ride. So I asked her and she said that she would love that but I would have to be patient because she was frightened of horses. That gave me a good laugh, her being frightened of horses. A pig will kill you if he sees a chance, but a horse is just like a great big baby. I told her I would teach her not to be scared of horses, I would teach her to ride horses. I told her I would modify her horse behaviour. That made her smile.

So that was how it started. From then on we had half our sessions in her nice little Cindy room with the flowers on the table, and half at the farm with the horses. She was not having me on about being scared of horses, but she did what she was told. Not a lot else she *could* do. It was a nice feeling, being in charge of her. Knowing she was trusting me to look after her. And she did trust me. She was at my mercy. I could do what I liked with her, when she was on that horse's back. I could have got her back broken or her neck broken if I'd felt like it. Do what I liked with her. Didn't want to hurt her though. It was nice, looking after her. I taught her to ride a horse. I modified her horse behaviour. Even had her galloping.

The first time she galloped, she was that scared. I made her walk Chucky right down to the end of the field, all on her own, then I made her turn him, and kick him up, so he ran flat out all the way back to where I was standing. I thought he wasn't going to stop for a second, but he did, and she slid right up his neck and then sort of slithered off, she was shaking all over, and she put her arms round my neck, and she kissed me, and I thought *yes*.

I think that was when I first got it set in my mind, what I would do.

One time, not long after the first time she galloped, she stayed for tea. My dad was talking on and on, trying to impress her, and all he was doing was making a bloody fool of himself. Whales, he was talking about; why is a whale like a whale and not like us. I ask you. Miss McLoughlin, Jo – I was calling her Jo by then, but only when she was at the farm – was trying to get Shirley to talk, but Shirley wouldn't say anything. She had this book, Shirley, *Sense and Sensibility* by Jane Austen, you could see Miss McLoughlin was surprised at her reading a book like that. Why shouldn't she read Jane Austen if she wants to? Just because she don't talk that doesn't mean she's bloody stupid. Then my bloody dad was off again.

'Books, horses. Bloody kids. Bloody holes in your bloody wallet. I often wonder, how did I come to be here on this bloody farm with all this lot? I'm a man who likes to think, Miss McLoughlin, see. Now I don't remember making no choices, yet here I am. And you know what my life feels like? Like being trapped in a bloody tunnel up to the neck in pigshit. So you tell me how that adds up.'

And she goes, 'I respect what you say about your feelings, Mr Bardsley, but surely there must be compensations?'

'Oh,' he goes, 'I don't see no compensations.' Bloody old fraud, I couldn't stand to hear another word of it.

'Yes, you bloody do,' I go. 'You tell her what they are, your compensations.' That shut him up. He picked up his fork and started eating again. '*I'll* tell her what they are, your compensations!' I go.

'Don't swear at the table, love.' That's my mother. First words she's said all tea-time.

'Well,' he goes. 'There you have it. All in all you might as well top yourself, right? I'm worth more dead than alive, I know that much.'

And I say, 'So why don't you bloody get on and do it, nobody here would shed no tears!'

It was not what you could call a nice conversation, but I was glad that she was there to hear it. Miss McLoughlin. Jo.

Back in school, Miss McLoughlin started asking me all these questions about Shirley, but I didn't tell her anything, I wasn't ready to tell her, if she didn't have the wit to sus it out for herself. I did tell her a bit about my hopes, though.

About how if he did top himself, or if they both just went away, how I could run that bloody place myself. Sell the pigs. Build up the milk round. Free-range eggs, build up that: Shirley would look after the chickens. Then get some ponies, build up the riding lessons. I told her how I'd got it all worked out in my head. I told her how it would be like bloody Paradise.

What she said, she said she believed me about how it would be, but that some things didn't look like changing, and all we could do was work small and neat with the things we could change.

I just laughed. Then I told her I loved her. She looked a bit worried when I said that, but I wasn't worried. I knew I could bring her round all right. She trusted me. I could do what I liked with her. She was my rubber dolly.

The next time she came to the farm, she was trying to be like she was the first time we met, like a hospital lady with a hospital smile and a look like a worried little girl behind that hospital smile. She started telling me about the contract, how it had worked out very well, and about how the reports on my behaviour in school were very encouraging, and about how in counselling it is often a good idea to agree on a date for termination of the work and stick to it, and that perhaps we had arrived at the time when we could fix a termination date.

I was so angry to hear her coming out with that load of pigshit that I gave Chucky a great smack on his arse, she was on him at the time, and he bolted with her, and serve her bloody well right, talking like that. At first I thought serve her bloody well right if she comes off and breaks her neck, but I didn't feel like that for long, I couldn't be angry with her; she was just a nervous little Cindy, just a little scared ratty girl who needed to be looked after and needed telling what was what. I went after her on Pedro and told her to head Chucky uphill if she could, she was hanging on like a good 'un, and she did that, and he slowed as he was coming to the top, and she got hold of him. She was just about in control I'd say by the time I got to her, but glad enough to slither off of him and have me hold her tight. My rubber dolly.

Afterwards I told her about Shirley. And how that's why she never said anything, because he told her never to say anything. Not even to the Hatton doctors. And my mum had never said anything about it either, she had just let it go on like it was one of the things she could not change. And she asked me, Miss McLoughlin, Jo, if he'd ever done it to me, and I said he'd tried it, but he left it a bit late; I was too fierce and nasty by then. Nearly bit his nose off. I told her I would never let any man touch me. Only her. Only her.

I loaded the gun, both barrels, while he was out doing the milk round, and I shot him as he was coming out of the barn. Just the one shot was all it took. And my mum came running out screaming and I turned the gun on her too. I was sorry to do that but it had to be done.

Then I cleaned the gun up and put it in his hand and I went in the house and waited with Shirley. I was waiting for her to come, Miss McLoughlin, Jo. My rubber dolly. When she saw I was not in school she would realise that something had happened and she would come to see if I was all right.

I had it all prepared what I would say.

'You heard him say he'd do it. Everyone round here has heard him say he'd top himself. We've got the farm now, me and Shirely. And I want you to come and live with us here. Help me look after Shirley. It'll be OK. You'll see. Shirley won't say anything. No need to worry about that. No need to worry about anything. You will stay, won't you? It'll be like Paradise. You will stay, won't you? Say you will. Say you will.'

That was what I was going to say to her.

Thanks Anyway

Lowlands University was initially something of a disappointment for Karl Blattman, and Karl Blattman was initially something of a disappointment for Lowlands University. The thing was, Karl was a Jane Austen man, and Jane Austen had actually visited with a sick cousin at Lowlands Rectory in 1814, gotten sick herself, and stayed quite a while. Karl hadn't expected everything to be there just as it was in Austen's day, but to track down the spot and find it covered with the only multi-storey car park in an English university was . . . well, it felt just a little cheap. And Lowlands University had thought it was getting rather a prestigious full professor from Ann Arbor on the exchange, not a two-bit associate professor from the much less prestigious (oh, let's be frank, not prestigious at all, diddleysquat cow college) Michigan State University, down the road from Ann Arbor in Ypsilanti. But Karl liked to see problems as opportunities in disguise, and Lowlands University was well used to making the best of a bad job.

Karl and Sally Anne arrived a week before the start of term. There was scarcely a soul to be seen except for a couple of nuns in a battered Mini driving out of the main car park past a No Exit sign. Sally Anne was a little thrown by this, but Karl explained to her that England had a great tradition of radical dissent.

'Radical dissenting *nuns*?' said Sally Anne, wrinkling her nose in that way she had, and Karl felt a sharp surge of lust. But Karl was a Jane Austen man, and Jane Austen men don't fuck in car parks in broad daylight, even with their wives. Sally Anne had not been Karl's wife for very long. His first, grindingly bitter marriage long over, he had resigned himself to the platonic service of the spinster from Steventon, until he found Sally Anne waiting tables with the bland contemptuous elegance of a young Chrissie Evert, in what might kindly be described as the Bohemian quarter of Ypsilanti. Karl felt himself very well served by Sally Anne. But there was something about Sally Anne which suggested that she was still waiting.

On the first day of term, Karl walked over to the Arts building, found his room, and was pounding the typewriter and puffing up a storm on his pipe by ten after eight. Lowlands being Lowlands, he was able to work on undisturbed, alone in the building, until half past nine, when a very tall thin man opened the door, stood in the doorway staring at him with what might have been horror, removed his vaguely clerical-looking spectacles as if to shield himself from too much fleshy reality, and said, 'Oh.'

'Hi there,' said Karl.

'Ah, of course,' said the tall man, sounding a little comforted. 'You must be Karl Blattman. I'm Arthur Fitzgerald. We, ah . . . share. This study, I mean.'

'Glad to meet you, Arthur,' said Karl, extending his thick stubby paw. 'Hope you don't mind the pipe.'

'Not at all,' said Arthur Fitzgerald. 'Murphy ate raw garlic,' he added obscurely, and before Karl could ask what Murphy had to do with anything, went on, 'd'you know, I've already had two extraordinary experiences this morning. The first was when I stopped to give someone a lift to the University . . . I'm not interrupting you, am I?'

'No, no. Go ahead,' said Karl. It was interesting to hear a new voice, and this one had such layered cadences, so unlike Sally Anne's flat transparent utterances.

His new colleague took three steps into the room, stared about him keenly, examined a very ordinary-looking chair with some suspicion for a few seconds; then he pulled it towards him firmly and perched on it, drawing his bony knees up to his chin and staring at Karl over them in a startled way, as if he was looking at a bear in a Donegal tweed jacket rather than a fellow-scholar.

'Well, she turned out to be one of ours. My passenger. In

the sense that she was an English student. Big angry eyes, fierce face, seemed somehow at loggerheads with things, you know, *that* sort, do you have them in the States? – I invited her into my modest Volkswagen, chauffered her impeccably, made pleasant conversation, and went out of my way to drop her *exactly* where she said she wanted to be. And when she got out of the car, do you know what she said? 'Well, thanks, anyway.' *Thanks, anyway*. as if despite all my efforts there was something inevitably disappointing about our encounter. Something . . . how shall I put it?'

'Ineluctably tragic?'

Arthur beamed at him.

'Exactly! Yes! Isn't it there, in those little hiccups of conversation, that the great sad truths leak out? It's all right. There you go. This is it. So, well. Thanks, anyway. Yes? And the other thing happened just afterwards. I was walking across the campus and happened to glance into one of the ground-floor flats. There, dancing serenely by herself, in her, um, underwear, her blonde hair tied on top of her head with a red hair ribbon, was an outstandingly beautiful young woman. I stopped. Our eyes met. She gave a sort of rueful smile, I a sort of hopeless shrug, and I passed on.'

'More ineluctable tragedy?'

'No, no, no. That was perfect. Nothing to spoil, d'you see?'

The English Department at Lowlands saw itself as the spiritual and moral heart of the University, the still point at the centre of Lowland's turning world. The rest of the University saw the English Department as hopelessly marginal. Lowlands, like any other British university in the eighties, was about real estate, cost-effectiveness, market viability, and the key departments were those which could deliver external funding at those sexy interfaces where pure research and business suddenly find themselves in intimate contact, sliding along each other's smooth surfaces, seeking the openings for fruitful interpenetration. Karl, coming from a place where English had always been marginal, could see that; could see, too, that he was a marginal member of a marginal department. Well, he could handle that. Karl was inner-directed, a self-starter. He came from farming stock, had had his own six cows at fourteen years old and handled them right. He liked to say that that had been a good preparation for small group teaching in the University and he was only half kidding. Lose one calf and that might be half a year's profit gone. Karl hated waste.

That was why he didn't awfully care for the way Professor Egerton talked about the weaker students, as if they were expendable, as if all they were good for was dogmeat. There was one who was mentioned at the Departmental meeting, a Miss Butcher, who was going to be Karl's personal student this year, if she survived her re-sits. Only Elwyn Price, the Departmental radical, had spoken up for her genuine but unsufficiently focussed talent, and Karl had found himself warming to the Welshman, and determined to pull this kid through. Where Karl came from, genuine talent was scarce as polar bear shit, and he wasn't about to waste a scrap of it.

Elwyn walked part of the way home with Karl, and waxed indignant about Egerton's coldness towards students and tightness with his hospitality allowance, contrasting this with the way he, Elwyn, had been treated on his visit to America.

'Like a bloody prince, man, a prince. Drinks, meals, wives. Like bloody Eskimos, it was heartwarming, to say the least.'

He started to go into detail about the Eskimo hospitality, and Karl, who didn't awfully care for that sort of thing, diverted the conversation back to University politics. Elwyn explained the faculty position: they were threatening to refuse to set and mark examinations in furtherance of their pay claim. If the faculty refused to set and mark examination, the students would not be able to graduate. This was, as Elwyn put it, the beauty of the scheme. Karl felt puzzled – was this the man who had spoken so warmly and tenderly in support of his students?

Elwyn put his arm round Karl's shoulders. 'Don't worry about it, man, it won't ever come to that. Just a move in the game. Just us trying to catch up a bit, starting to live in the twentieth century.'

'I kind of hoped it would be different here,' said Karl.

The Vice-Chancellor, a very small man called Ernest Hemmingway, gave a party to which Karl and Sally Anne were invited, though it was not a welcoming party and they were not the guests of honour. The news that Michigan State was not Ann Arbor, nor ever would be, had hit the Vice-Chancellor hard, and Karl got the strong impression that as far as the Vice-Chancellor was concerned, he was somehow the wrong kind of American.

Deirdre Hemmingway asked Sally Anne what she did in the States and Sally Anne said, 'Wait tables, I guess.' The Vice-Chancellor's wife thought she was talking about atomic weight tables and confessed to being a bit of a fool about nuclear physics. Sally Anne explained that nuclear physics didn't really come into it; people would tell her what they wanted to eat and she would bring it to the table and then they would eat it. Deirdre Hemmingway said that she had often thought what an interesting job that must be. Sally Anne said that it was sure as shit more interesting than hanging round on campus being a faculty wife. And as Deirdre Hemmingway had devoted more than half her lifetime to hanging round campus being a faculty wife, Sally Anne was given the strong impression that *she* was the wrong kind of American too.

Elwyn Price, who was drunk, assured her that she was exactly the right kind of American as far as he was concerned, and that what he would like to do more than anything in the world at that moment was to put his hand down her dress and feel her lovely tits. Sally Anne invited him in her clear flat carrying voice to go ahead and feel her lovely tits if it meant so much to him, and Elwyn swivelled his head round this way and that and then emitted a long and desperately hearty laugh for the benefit of the dozen or so people who were listening. Sally Anne walked into the garden, where she had a short and mutually satisfactory conversation with Arthur Fitzgerald, whom she had seen watching her doing her exercises that first day of term.

One Wednesday morning a few weeks later, Karl was sitting in the office he shared with Arthur Fitzgerald, puffing up a storm and pounding the keys, when the door opened and he looked up to see a girl of about twenty with wild curly hair staring at him with what looked like angry accusation. She was, it turned out, Liz Butcher, his problem personal student, making her first official appearance of the term, having had, as she told Karl, some trouble in getting herself together. With very little prompting she went on to tell him that this trouble was not unconnected with Tim Murphy, his phantom *doppelgänger*, the man at whose desk he was now sitting.

'I'm such a pushover,' she said. 'He told me I was very talented, and I believed him, but it was only because he wanted to screw me, and yes, he did, and then that got too *heavy* for him . . . what a bastard – am I shocking you?'

'No, I guess these things happen in Michigan too,' said Karl.

'Yes, I'll bet they do,' she said bitterly. 'Especially if Tim Murphy's there.'

'I guess that must have hurt quite a lot,' said Karl.

'Well, he didn't have to run away as far as America,' said Liz Butcher, starting to cry.

At this point the door opened and Arthur Fitzgerald came in, hesitating elaborately.

'Ah. Hello, ah . . . *Liz*. Sorry, Karl. Yes, of course, silly of me. It's Wednesday, isn't it? You're teaching in here all morning, aren't you?'

'I guess so, Arthur,' said Karl.

'Of course. Well, I'll just, ah . . . fine.'

When he had gone, Karl told Liz Butcher that he had read her work and that he thought she had talent too, and that he had no ulterior motive at all for saying so. He told her that she had talent, and she was wasting it, and he told her how he felt about waste, and talent, and polar bear shit, and the six cows he had had when he was fourteen, and pretty soon he had Liz Butcher agreeing to a programme of work which involved going to all lectures and seminars, even the optional ones, and 8 am private tutorials with Karl every Wednesday and Friday.

Arthur Fitzgerald walked round to Karl and Sally Anne's apartment and rang the bell. Sally Anne took a little while to answer the door, and when she opened it Arthur was a little taken aback to see that she was pink, wet, and wearing only a light green towel. It seemed that he had chosen an inconvenient time to call, but then, after a few moments, it became clear that it was quite convenient after all.

And yes, yes, I do really think that's all you need just there, anything else would be to warp and falsify because neither of them ever really understood what it was and if I am to be honest I must say that I doubt if any of us ever really do understand what it is . . . Sally Anne in a strange country, unable to work, unable to study, her husband's back like a thick black stone as he pounded the keys behind a cloud of pipesmoke, disguising his fear of her needs as a slab of virtue. Sally Anne, intrigued by Arthur's hesitant birdy overtures, his delicate hints at harmonies unguessed at in Kentucky meadows . . . he in his turn responding to her clear certainties, her flat blond enthusiasms, thinking perhaps here, if anywhere, is life, the thing itself . . . is that how it was, or was it more, or less? And though I would love to sound the thrilling deep notes of MORE, of COURSE it was MORE, MORE, INCOMPARABLY MORE, they felt it BLOSSOM in the DEEP HEART'S CORE . . . oh, it makes you feel so wonderful and grand, but can't we please admit the truth, a little bit uncomfortable as well: there's something very appealing after all about the steady flat drip of less . . . less . . . less.

Not that motivation is the only thing, dear God no; some of us feel more at home with tactile immediacy . . . well, we have her blondness, we have her warm damp pinkness pleasingly contrasted with the fluffy peppermint green towel, oh, we could dally with the heartbreakingly beaky tenderness of the way his thin body arches over her sturdy tennis-player's back, etcetera, but even Keats must finally have wearied of loading every rift with ore from his frigged-to-a-frazzle imagination . . . oh, all right, if you insist, one little detail: after he had come, with his characteristic whimper that carried the cadence of a lengthy adverbial clause of concession,

she liked to lie with her arms round his thin shanks, holding
his slack spent penis, pale and delicate as a mushroom stalk,
in her mouth, just holding it gently there, like a little girl
sucking her thumb, getting and giving simple and unequivo-
cal comfort. And he would think about that years later, and
wish he had paid more attention at the time.

'So,' said Karl Blattman, lecturing on *Emma*, 'she continues
to entertain the idea of being in love with him, and he with
her. Entertain the idea, that's what she says. What else is
there for her to do in Highbury but entertain ideas? Maybe
the less choice you have, the more it stimulates your imagination. When my parent were kids, there were just four or five
families within visiting distance. Folk had to make their
hopes fit what was there. And maybe for some people it's not
really so different now.'

And the academic year slouched on: Christmas, Spring. Karl
continued to get to his desk every day by eight am, Arthur
Fitzgerald continued to visit Sally Ann Blattman every Wednesday morning. The lecturers' pay dispute smouldered and
sputtered and the threat to boycott examinations was not
withdrawn. Electronic surveillance equipment was installed
in the library and Liz Butcher was caught in it. Karl persuaded
the librarian not to press charges against her, and succeeded
in defending her at the next Department Meeting, rather to
the amusement of some of his colleagues.

'You mean Egerton thinks I'm *screwing* Liz Butcher?' he said
as he and Elwyn walked back across the campus past a couple
of damp sociologists playing with a Frisbee.
  'Well, what did you think all that was about her "efforts
giving you so much pleasure"?'
  'You mean that's what *everyone* assumes?'
  'Look, don't get me wrong, Karl. I identify. Any good
teacher has got to be open, wide open ... knowledge has no
bloody boundaries, we let them take what they need from us,
we're not mean with ourselves. I respect that Karl. Not many
of us have got it to give, after all. Eh?'
  He patted Karl on the shoulder.

'Look, Elwyn,' said Karl, hearing his voice a little unsteady. 'It isn't so. I'm really sorry to disappoint everyone.'

'Oh,' said Elwyn. 'Right. Sorry. Fine. Ah . . . how's that lovely wife of yours then?'

'Still lovely, I guess,' said Karl.

'What we want to do,' said Elwyn, 'is get away from this place for a day, expand, breathe a bit of air. You been to Avebury yet? Megan is nutty about all that stuff. Standing stones, primitive magic. All crap, of course, but it's a lovely excuse for a bit of open-air drinking. We'll all go. Sunday?'

'Sunday would be fine I guess,' Karl said, thinking that it would in truth be good to get off campus and into some real country.

'We'll have a picnic,' said Elwyn, his clear blue boozer's eyes alight. 'Megan adores a bloody picnic. Wives, kids, wine, chicken. You can bring that girl you're not screwing, as well. Come on, man, the least you can give her is a ham roll, right?'

'Nature,' said Karl Blattman, lecturing on *Emma*, 'seems to pose some sort of threat to Jane Austen's people. The heat makes them cross, or ill. They catch cold in the rain. Most of all, maybe, something seems to slacken the stiffening, melt all that glue that sticks little society together. People don't change a lot. Maybe they're just more themselves. And that's not nice.'

They went in two cars. Elwyn and Megan Price, with the two boys in the back, led the way. Karl and Sally Anne followed with Arthur Fitzgerald and Liz Butcher. Megan would be the first to admit that she was not the world's best navigator, and her task was complicated by the fact that the Ordnance Survey maps tend to omit the Old Straight Tracks. After driving in circles for some miles Elwyn had had enough, and jammed his big old Citroën up a lane at the foot of a little hill.

'Right! That's bloody it! I don't care where we bloody are! I want my bloody picnic!'

'Looks like a nice place, Elwyn,' said Karl.

But Megan was standing staring up the hill, her eyes as wide as a little girl's.

'It's *the* place!' she cried. 'That's not a hill, that's a tumulus. We've really found it. It really is the place. It's like magic. A tumulus on high ground, with a fringe of woods at the base.'

'Like a hairy nipple,' said Elwyn. 'Come on, let's get up there and get the bottles open.'

'I brought too much food,' said Megan half an hour later. 'I always do.'

'No, no,' said Karl comfortably. 'Can't have too much food on a picnic. Real nice, here, Megan. Real peaceful spot.'

'Can you feel it then?' said Megan eagerly.

'Well, sure,' said Karl, a little puzzled. 'I feel fine, Megan.'

'That's good,' she said meaningfully. Elwyn groaned.

'Go on then,' he said. 'Tell him why he feels fine.'

'We're very near to a crossing of the ley lines here,' said Megan. Her eyes were shining. 'The Old Straight Tracks. They go back before history. Really, thousands of them, all over England. They're straighter and longer than the Roman roads, and hardly anyone knows about them. You can see how they link up standing stones and tumuli hundreds of miles away from each other. And they're still here, Karl. They're . . . underneath everything!'

'That right?' said Karl uneasily.

'She's been reading Alfred Watkins,' Arthur explained. 'You see, Sally Anne, all those twisty roads and dead ends you've been complaining about are just there to confuse you. Underneath, we're as straight as a die.'

'Kind of a prehistoric freeway system?'

'Oh, no, Sally Anne, it's much more than that,' said Megan eagerly. 'They had a religious function too, and they harnessed sources of energy.'

'Like North Sea bloody oil, you see,' said Elwyn. 'Oh, God. Let me lie in your lap, Liz.'

'You what?' said Liz, squinting into the sun.

'I mean with my head in your lap.'

'You'd better,' she said.

'Dad's pissed,' said Tim Price, his younger son, gratuitously.

'And the thing is,' Megan went on determinedly, for Karl at least was still listening courteously, 'that here, somewhere

134

just below us in the woods there, there's a meeting of three of these ley lines. There ought to be some sort of markstone, but even if that's gone – well they say people can feel it, actually *feel* the sources of energy.'

They were all staring at her.

'And . . . I just think it would be nice if we could find the place, that's all, and . . . see what it was like.'

After a short pause, Elwyn said,' If you are wondering whether this woman is deranged, I can't blame you. This is what sixteen years of being a university wife does to a woman.'

'Sixteen years of you, you mean,' she said.

'Right!' said Elwyn. 'She's in flight from reality. Look. This is real. This grass. This . . . may I, Liz? . . . this foot. This warm, dirty, plump, wonderful foot. That bloody comic the kids are reading. What's here and now. That's all we've got. Everyone else knows that, *you* know that, why can't it be enough for you? Why can't you just sit on the tump with the rest of us and drink a bit of wine in the sun? Because you're in flight from bloody reality, that's why!'

There were tears in her eyes.

'It's all right, Karl. Really. Just a bit of warm family life, this is,' she said.

'Well,' said Karl, 'I think I'd like to help you look for that markstone.'

'Hell, why not?' said Sally Anne. 'After all that food and wine I could really use a source of, what was it, primal energy?'

'You don't need a source of primal energy, you *are* a source of primal energy,' said Elwyn.

It seemed natural enough that the seekers after the source of primal energy should split into teams of two. Sally Anne Blattman plunged plunged briskly into the thickest part of the wood, drawing Arthur Fitzgerald after her. Karl Blattman and Megan Price, being more contemplative and less active in temperament, or perhaps because they both had short legs, wandered more slowly along the winding paths. Liz Butcher needed to have a pee, and though she vehemently refused Elwyn Price's offer to stand guard, he followed her anyway.

135

Tim and Moelwyn Price stayed on the tumulus reading comics.

It was very cool and still under the trees. By the time they had been walking for half an hour Karl and Megan could hear nothing of the others, only the birdsong and the faint hum of the distant traffic, though they were still within sight of the tumulus.

'I guess these woods must be really old,' said Karl.

'Oh, the *woods* aren't old,' she said. 'The stone would have been here long before all these trees and stuff. That's why it's so . . . it should show up white, but maybe after all these years it's got buried under . . . there is one thing we could try.'

'What's that?'

'Well I know it sounds silly, but they say if you put your ear to the ground you can hear the current under the earth. The energy source. You have to lie down with your head on the earth sort of thing.'

'Is that so?' said Karl, a little uneasily.

'Shall we try?'

'Er . . . right here?'

'It doesn't hurt, you know, Karl.'

They lay down on the mossy earth.

'It's supposed to be better if you're in physical contact,' said Megan after a few moments.

'Er, right.'

After another few minutes, Karl said, 'Megan.'

'What is it, Karl?'

'I guess I don't feel any of that energy flow, you know.'

'Don't you?'

'Sorry,' he said. 'I feel kind of stupid lying here. I guess I'm going to get up now, Megan.'

'Yes, all right, Karl,' she said.

He heaved himself up, and offered her his hand. As she stood up, she stumbled against him, then stiffened in his arms.

'Karl!'

'What?'

'There! Through the bushes! I think it's the markstone! Can't you see? Shining white, over there!'

Karl looked. There indeed was something white, catching dappled patterns of light through the leaves; a tallish slender rounded white boulder . . . He caught his breath.

'Oh, no,' she said crossly. 'It isn't anything after all. It's only people.'

He sat with his face to the wall, typing, his pipe in his mouth, his shoulders hunched, his back like a big dark boulder to her.

'Karl?' she said. 'What are you trying to do? Are you trying to wipe me out or what?'

'I'm trying to work,' he said.

'Why don't you talk to me?'

'I don't have anything to say,' he said. He stopped typing. 'All right. I hurt. Is that what you want to hear?'

'No,' she said. 'I don't want you to hurt. But I can't close myself down, Karl.'

'Then leave me alone and let me work. OK?'

She looked at his back for a few moments.

'OK.'

Spring shuffled shyly into summer in that way it had at Lowlands. The local branch of the Association of University Teachers passed a resolution to refuse to cooperate in the invigilation and marking of examinations. The Vice-Chancellor requested chairmen of departments to submit to him a list of all faculty members participating in this action, and Professor Egerton called an extraordinary meeting of the English Department. Elwyn Price outlined the strategy.

'We're going to meet this head-on. Refuse to cooperate. Black the blacklist. And there's going to be a day of action on Wednesday week. A total withdrawal of all academic staff. Cancel all lectures, all tutorials, the lot.'

'Day of inaction, so to speak?'

'Oh, don't be so bloody stupid, Arthur. We have a working agreement with the Students' Union for full support and cooperation.'

'I know,' said Professor Egerton, 'that many people like

137

myself find this sort of thing rather distasteful. But I think we must all feel bound by the Association's decision. Fortunately, perhaps, not very many of us actually have a teaching commitment on a Wednesday morning.'

He looked around the room.

'I do,' said Karl.

Egerton sighed, barely audibly.

'And I really don't like to be pushy and awkward about this, but I guess I'm not bound by your union's decisions. I think I ought to tell you I'll be going to work on Wednesday week.'

'Curious how everyone's vocabulary at these meetings ossifies into little abstract chunks,' said Arthur as he and Karl walked past the lake towards the University flats. 'Total withdrawal, full cooperation, academic freedom . . . imagine trying to draw a picture of academic freedom for a Martian visitor . . . Look, Karl, I really do think you should reconsider about Wednesday week. Couldn't you have your students round at your flat, informally? You see, all this is just part of the game, you must see that. Doing the right thing at this point might turn out to be terribly complicated and damaging, d'you see? *Do* you see?'

'Yeah, I guess my stance is kind of ludicrous,' said Karl. 'But how I see it – if Elwyn Price has the academic freedom to withold his brilliance from his students, I guess I've got the right to go in and bore the pants off mine, same as any other Wednesday.'

Arthur stopped, and smiled. '*That's* what it was. I knew I'd been hearing a familiar tune, but it was the American harmonies that confused me. Karl, you're an anachronism. You're an authentic nineteenth-century hero.'

'Oh, no. Just a noble savage.'

Somehow, Arthur didn't quite like the way Karl was looking at him.

'And what do you plan to do on Wednesday week, Arthur?'

'Oh . . . easy for me. I . . . have no commitments on Wednesday mornings, Karl.'

'Yeah, that's right. You don't. I teach all Wednesday mornings. While you're . . .'

'Free.'
'Right.'

A couple of days after that, Karl came home from work to find Ernest Hemmingway, the Vice-Chancellor, sitting on his couch in tennis shorts sipping a martini. He had, it seemed, received a little allocation of garden party invitations, from Buckingham Palace, and Deirdre had immediately thought of Karl and Sally Anne.

'Well, that's really kind of you, Vice-Chancellor . . .'

'Ernie, please. Think nothing of it. Great pleasure. Wednesday week. I'll lay on one of the University cars for you. Save the, er, hassle, eh?'

'I teach on Wednesdays, Ernie,' said Karl slowly.

'My dear chap,' said Hemmingway, 'that'll be all right. Special occasion. In any case, isn't there some sort of boycott business on Monday?'

'Yes, there is, but I've arranged to meet my classes as usual.'

'Oh, dear,' said the Vice-Chancellor. 'I wonder whether there's any way round this. You see, the thing is, I've already mentioned this to Mrs Blattman, and she did seem rather keen, I thought.'

'Is that so? Well, sure, she can go on her own if she wants to,' said Karl.

Ernest Hemmingway stared searchingly at Karl through the strings of his oversize Prince tennis racquet.

'That wasn't really what I meant, Karl,' he said, frowning and rubbing his little round nose against the strings. 'You see, there is rather a delicate situation here.'

'I've had it explained to me,' said Karl.

'Good, good. I often think it must be terribly difficult for a visitor to understand the way things work here.'

'Well, I don't know,' said Karl. 'The more I see, the more it seems like the way things work at Michigan State.'

'Where you still haven't got your full professorship.'

'Yeah, right. It was real kind of you to think of us, Ernie. But, you know, I don't think Buckingham Palace would be my scene.'

'No, no, fine, fine,' said the Vice-Chancellor, and then, a

shade petulantly, 'one does rather wonder what your scene might be, Karl.'

'Teaching and research, Ernie. That's all. I'm really sorry to disappoint everyone.'

The following Wednesday, Karl Blattman put on his best suit and walked to the Arts building to teach his classes. A number of people were there to see him do it, including Elwyn Price, who was there in his official capacity as a union picket, and Arthur Fitzgerald, who had gone, so to speak, as himself. Arthur Fitzgerald was reminded of the climax of *On the Waterfront*, in which Marlon Brando defied the union bosses and staggered into work, bloody but unbowed. All that was needed was the right music, and for Karl's legs to be a little longer. Elwyn Price told Arthur Fitzgerald to grow up, and pointed out that *On The Waterfront* was in any case an ideologically suspect movie. By this time, Karl was coming up the steps, and Elwyn stepped into his path.

'Hi, Elwyn,' said Karl.

'This is an official picket of the Association of University Teachers, backed by the National Union of Students,' said Elwyn. 'May I ask where you're going?'

'Oh, come on, Elwyn,' said Karl. 'This is me. You know where I'm going. I'm going into the faculty and I'm going to do some work, OK?'

'You know you're in violation of a unanimous agreement?'

'Can't be unanimous without everyone,' said Karl. 'Now, come on, Elwyn, this is kind of embarrassing.'

'It's a bloody sight worse than that!' said Elwyn, abruptly abandoning his official style. 'I didn't think you'd do it, boy, I really didn't think you'd do it. Scratch an American and find a Facist – I didn't believe it before but, by God, I bloody do now!'

'Well, you know, Elwyn,' said Karl in an irritatingly good-tempered way, 'right now I don't give a pinch of soured owl-shit for what you think, I just want to go to work.'

Opinions differ about precisely what happened next. Some observers maintain that Dr Price struck at Dr Blattman, but slipped and missed his footing. Others are sure that Dr Blattman pushed Dr Price to the ground by walking into him. All agree on the essential facts: that Dr Blattman crossed the picket and went into work, and that Dr Price finished up on his hands and knees, shouting after Dr Blattman:

'You bloody traitor! We haven't finished with you yet!'

'I do love a closely argued debate,' said Arthur Fitzgerald, and, as Elwyn did not answer to this, 'well, Wednesday being my free morning, I think I'll toddle off.'

When Karl arrived in the classroom he was not too surprised to find that the only student there was Liz Butcher. He was, however, surprised when she took advantage of the situation to tell him that she was in love with him, and he was even more surprised when she proposed that instead of discussing *Mansfield Park*, they should take off their clothes and make love. Liz Butcher, on the other hand, was not all that surprised when Karl told her that while he appreciated her offer very much, he felt that it would be a shame to fall behind schedule on the Jane Austen programme after they had made such good progress. But to show that there were no hard feelings, and that he was not, contrary to rumour, so tight that you couldn't drive a mustard seed up his ass with a sledge hammer, he produced a pint of Jim Beam from the middle drawer of his desk to help them through the stickier passages.

So that's it? That's what we're saying here? Arthur indulged, while Karl nobly restrained himself? Is this a temperance tract of the academic life? Teaching and research are the proper concerns of the academic, teaching and research within one's own narrow academic field, that is. The teaching of new forms of dalliance, research into the softnesses of one's colleagues' wives and loved ones, these are not permissible activities for the University teacher of English language and literature. Who is, in this text as in (regrettably) so many others, assumed to be male (though examples of the contrary abound, even at Lowlands). Oh, yes, we seem to be talking about boys' games again, and the women are perceived as daughters of those games, light-heeled and voiceless ... or to put it another way, mysterious, unknowable. Isn't it strange? I'm much shyer about trying to get inside her head than I ever was about getting inside her body. It seems an intolerable intrusion. Let them write their own texts. This one is mine, and I feel duty bound to the truth as I see it, which is that women are a snare and a delusion, a glittering distraction from man's proper pursuits. There.

Arthur Fitzgerald went round to Karl and Sally Anne's flat and broke off the relationship in terms that are too shaming and embarrassing to go into detail about here . . . oh, well, if you absolutely must have more than that: she was innocently pleased to see him and completely missed his careful indicators that all was not well; she was not to be put off by his talk of Karl and the damage the relationship was doing to Arthur's friendship with him; she spoke much and angrily about bullshit and demanded to know where Arthur was coming from, and he started to giggle and say he was coming from Tunbridge Wells; with a wild and hopeless whiff of burnt boats in his nostrils he found himself telling her that he had never been able to think of Sally Anne as a real name, never really been able to see its owner as a real person, and at their most intimate moments, at the very moments when . . . I can't say it, I can't say it, at those moments, you *know* those moments, moments of total abandonment, exposure, loneliness, *particularly* at those moments, though at others as well, he had felt that he was making love to a very beautifully made inflatable doll oh God oh God oh God forgive me Sally Anne forgive me God as well.

Sally Anne thanked Arthur Fitzgerald for his honesty. And she thanked him for trying so hard all the time: it must have been, she felt, quite a performance. She told him (and whether she was telling the truth or not is anyone's guess) that he was the worst lay she had had in her whole life. And then she told him to get the fuck out.

As an exchange professor, Karl Blattman was scheduled to deliver a public lecture in the summer term, and he continued to work on this, even though there was an official boycott on all his lectures and classes. He intended to deliver it, even if

142

no one at all turned up, though he suspected that the odd freak might come along out of curiosity. He was, in his own way, happy. Sally Anne had come back to him; he didn't know why and he didn't ask. He was her friend and she was his friend.

One week before the lecture was due to take place, he received a telegram from Ann Arbor, offering him a post there as full professor, the appointment to be taken up immediately. Smelling a rat, he went to see the Vice-Chancellor, and found him by the croquet lawn, watching Deirdre make mincemeat of a couple of Ghanaian diplomats.

'Oh, yes,' said Hemmingway, 'I had heard it on the grapevine, absolutely splendid news, though no more than you deserve, of course, with your excellent publications. Now. I gather that Ann Arbor particularly want you for the summer semester, they're practically making a condition of it, and in the circumstances of course we won't make any difficulties about that here.'

'Well, I haven't decided to take the job yet,' said Karl.

'Of course, it's entirely your own decision,' said the Vice-Chancellor, 'but I can't imagine a better offer, Karl, can you?'

'We did talk about the possibility of my staying on here.'

'Well, you have become rather a problem, haven't you?' said Hemmingway, throwing his fat little arm as far as he could around Karl's broad shoulders. 'In confidence, we're very close to a retrospective agreement with the UGC, it's a very delicate time in particular and in general for the universities, and this continued boycott of your course . . . quite wrongheaded in my opinion, but there it is, and it is so much the sort of thing that appeals to our dreadful newspapers, so much less mature and responsible than yours . . . I personally find your independence enormously appealing, Karl, but, well . . . there you have it.'

'I'm a problem,' said Karl.

'Through no fault of your own. And, in confidence, when someone becomes a problem through no fault of their own, sometimes we're able to solve it by giving them something, and at other times, to put it crudely, we have to solve it by taking something away from them. And I'm absolutely delighted that this opportunity has come just at the right time for you. D'you follow?'

'Yes,' said Karl. 'I just wanted it spelt out, I guess.'

'Bye, Karl!' shouted Deirdre. 'Do come back and see us!'

Ernest Hemmingway was only too sorry that he wasn't able to get along to Karl's public lecture, which was entitled 'Jane Austen and the Lost Ley Lines'. Not many other people were able to get along either. Liz Butcher. A couple of nuns. Arthur Fitzgerald. Sally Anne. Nobody else that Karl recognised. Karl didn't mind too much. He had some things that he wanted to say, and he had been able to say them, and now he was nearly done.

'Finally, though,' said Karl, 'for all the brilliance and gaiety on the surface of Austen's novels, all that sense of life and life's possibilities, what wells up underneath, in every story, is a tragic sense of loss and disillusionment. Loss of innocence, sometimes, loss of confidence or will, loss of individual freedom, as one by one those heroines acknowledge their mistakes, and settle for the comfortable second best that society affords them.'

He paused, and one of the nuns coughed.

'Well, now, having laid all that on you, having cast a pall of Midwestern gloom over the funniest writer in the English language, a language I like to think we share, just one final thought on those lost moral ley lines. Coming here from the States, I'd hoped to find that English moral tradition, if not intact, at least nagging away on the sidelines. But it wasn't so. As your Vice-Chancellor wisely pointed out to me, we are all Americans now.'

He cleared his throat, as if he had more to say, but then, as if he had changed his mind, he smiled a brief vague smile and walked off the platform.

'Well,' said Arthur Fitzgerald in the car park. 'Ah . . . all set, so to speak.'

'Yeah,' said Karl. 'Thanks for the roof rack. We seem to be taking home a lot more than we brought with us.'

'As it were . . . Er, curious how . . . I wish one had been able to . . . forms of language are so inadequate.'

'Just say "you have a good trip now, Karl and Sally Anne",' said Sally Anne.

'You have a good trip now, Karl and Sally Anne,' said Arthur.

'There,' she said. 'See? It's easy. And mind you come and see us, you hear me?'

She was, Arthur felt, tormenting him deliberately.

'Yes,' he said. 'Yes. If I'm . . . you know.'

Karl started the motor.

'Hey, Arthur!'

'What?'

'Thanks, anyway.'

Lowlands
March, '90.

Dear 'Karl',

Frightfully difficult. I've been sitting here for half an hour wondering how to start this. But, well, anyway, I did feel that you (and 'Sally Anne', if she is so inclined) should have the chance of glancing over the enclosed *short fiction* before it edges shyly into the spotlight, so to speak. And I hope you will forgive those little elisions through which one has attempted to render life into art. I found it very liberating, if I may say so, to invade and inhabit your sturdy frame for a while, albeit merely as a narrative strategist in the loose impersonal mode.

I am, as you see, still here, though the English Department has long since been subsumed into Communication Sciences. Increasingly, as time passes, I am prey to the feeling that I understand nothing at all of what is going on in the world.

No hard feelings, I trust, and, well,

Thanks, anyway,
'Arthur'.

Ann Arbor
April, '90.

'Arthur',

Good to hear from you and to read your text. It is *your text*, 'Arthur', and both of us thought how English and how like you it was. Both of us thought, too, that it was kind of cute the way you made us husband and wife instead of going straight for the father-daughter thing. I guess reality was always a little rich for your blood, right? Or was that just your English tact?

Kidding aside, both of us got pretty much what we wanted out of our year in Europe, and we are both grateful for what you were able to do for us and we aren't about to beef about what you couldn't do. 'Sally Anne' in particular wants to stress this: she says to remember that you were, after all, just her Wednesday morning man.

Both of us realised at the time that I was the one you really wanted to get into. And now, in a sense, you have. Well:

'You're welcome'.

'Karl'.

Travelling

Ever since he could remember, Dore had liked to travel by train. He liked almost everything about it. He liked getting to the station early, strolling over to the glass window to buy his ticket, then loitering at the bookstall, checking the value of his car in the motor magazines, choosing a different newspaper from the one they delivered to his home, and finding in this an almost adulterous satisfaction: he had always been a man for fine detail. Small deviations were enough to excite him. He never glanced, for example, at the pornographic magazines or the paperback novels in the Adult Reading section. Not at his local station, anyway. Then to the buffet, where he would buy a large tea in a takeaway container and sit nursing it, so that half would still be left when the train came. He found great pleasure in this.

In a perverse way he liked to get to the station late as well, relishing the ecstatic fumble for coins in the Pay And Display car park, the fine agonies of the queue, which might yield such exquisite torture as an elderly lady who had lost her cheque book, a pair of Japanese back-packers demanding arcane concessionary fares in unintelligible accents, while Dore hopped from foot to foot behind them, knowing with a desperate little thrill of certainty that the Intercity train for London Euston was already sliding its heavy inexorable bulk along the length of Platform One. Gabbling his order, grabbing his ticket, he would burst through the barrier, clutch at a closing door, stumble up the aisle, and sink panting, sighing, triumphant, into his seat.

Once under way, it was the passivity he liked. The pleasure of letting his eyes go out of focus, even close for minutes at

149

a time. Opening his briefcase and letting the reports and agenda slide out. Making his coarse marks on their smooth surfaces. Bundling them away. Taking out the newspaper and going through it like a dose of salts, taking pleasure in folding it carelessly, creasing and crumpling it, finally crushing it, abandoning it, forgetting it. Looking out of the window. Canals. Barges. Fields. Factories. A stretch of motorway, the rain-soaked dirty cars straining and struggling away through their tunnel of oily spray in the fast lane, their drivers hunched at the wheel, while he spread himself, yawned, picked his teeth. He liked to stroll down the train and get himself a drink. He enjoyed visiting the toilet, particularly if he could go in immediately after an attractive woman. He would sniff the odours that lingered after her, and imagine how she had pulled down her pants and spread her soft white bottom on the seat. Then he would use it himself, shake off the drops while watching himself in the mirror, zip up his trousers and walk back down the aisle, smiling to himself. He sometimes wondered what he would say if anyone asked him why he was smiling, but no one ever did.

Now he had been voted on to the National Executive he needed to be in London two or three times a week. Some of the meetings were in Bloomsbury, and some of them were in West London. The Union was very good about expenses, and made no difficulties about his staying the night in a hotel as often as he wanted to. Nothing too plushy of course: the Russell and the Tavistock were about the mark, and handy for Fettle House, the Union Headquarters, and for the station. But generally he found himself catching the train back in the evening. He was fond of his wife, and he liked to spend the night in his own bed; that was what he said, and it was true as far as it went. But there was more to it than that. Hotels made him feel strange. Anxiety in the foyer, yes, and apprehension in the lift, and worries about the key, and doubts about tipping; yes, all that.

But for him, there was more. When he was alone in the bedroom with the door shut, on his own, private, it was as if he did not know what to do with himself. More than that, he was not sure how to be himself. He could not tell whether he was hungry, or thirsty, or sleepy. He did not know whether he wanted to sit in a chair or lie on the bed. He did not know whether he was lonely or content with his own company. He did not know whether he wanted the TV on or not. When he stayed in a hotel he would often spend six hours or more in this state of suspended animation, until he was no longer sure of what it meant to be him. And when finally he slipped between the sheets, turned off the light, and cupped his hand round his cock for comfort, it felt to him like the hand of a stranger.

Dore was fifty years old and a father of daughters, but he did not feel himself to be well versed in women. Apart from a brief and rather painful interlude with a woman at work, he had been a faithful husband. The cheerful badinage that seemed to come so easily to other men did not come easily to him. Women seemed to him a rather serious matter; there was something daunting about them, even (he realised when he thought about it) his own wife and daughters. He had not been privy to their women's secrets; he did not really know what, well, what made them tick. The phrase seemed apt. They did tick mysteriously away, like Swiss clocks, or time-bombs. 'All right, Daddy. It's nothing to do with you.'

He felt innocent. He looked rather innocent, too, his skin smooth for a man of his age, his lips full and soft. When he looked at himself in the mirror he felt it strange that his sexual life had come to an end. But that was what seemed to be the case. For some time now he had felt increasingly reluctant to invade his wife's compliant but all too clearly indifferent body; and the business with the woman at work had not, of course, helped. His wife, by a series of hints and allusions, had indicated to him that it was not unusual, it was indeed accepted practice, for a married couple's sex life to come gradually to a sedate and graceful halt at ... well, now she came to think of it, at round about the age at which they found themselves now ...

He looked around at the couples who formed their acquaintance – they had no intimate friends – and, though he could not be sure, it seemed to him that what his wife said might well be true. Why, then, did he feel as if he had barely started? What was he going to do about it? They were questions that could be answered quickly, if gloomily. He had always been too unsure of himself to be the kind of man who seized the moment, and he was not going to change now. He had, it seemed, chosen his fate, and he was going to have to live with it.

Not that his life was miserable. 'Mustn't grumble,' was what he said when people asked him how it was going, and indeed he felt that he had no right to grumble. His wife and daughters seemed fond of him and rather proud of him in their mild way; after years of having to be careful he was now earning considerably more than his family's modest needs required; he was extremely highly regarded by his colleagues for his ability to research and analyse a problem: he would provide the solid grounds of evidence on which they could exercise their more flamboyant skills of argument and rhetoric. He found the work itself deeply absorbing and satisfying; what was more, he was doing something to help his fellow men, or at least those of his fellow men whose employment lay in the engineering sector.

Yet at the end of a day in London he would often find himself restless, unsatisfied, walking the narrow streets between Leicester Square and Oxford Street, streets full of loners like himself, breathing that thick air that had been breathed by so many already, the dazzling red and green of neon signs reflecting off the hard eyes of strangers. Nude glossy reddish-brown ducks revolving slowly in the windows of Chinese restaurants, the air full of the smell of cooked flesh. People eating in the street, the black holes of their mouths opening, teeth clamping and tearing at meaty kebabs and hamburgers, red sauce glittering at the corners of their lips. Signs above doorways promising LIVE SHOWS TEN GIRLS TEN AND THEY REALLY MOVE . . . the signs so bright and the doorways so dark . . . Some of them had photographs outside: young women of about the same age as his daughters thrusting their bottoms and their cunts towards his face . . . was this what he wanted? He could not bring himself to enter, he could not bring himself to enter even a restaurant, he did not know whether he was hungry, thirsty, whether he craved sex, love, oblivion . . . On and on he would walk, often covering the same ground several times, until baffled, tired, and still unsatisfied, he would resign himself to the late train from Euston or the single room in Tavistock Square.

More often than not it was the late train. The late train was a very different affair from the trains he caught in the morning. There were jolly parties clutching glossy souvenir programmes from concerts and musicals, anxiously raucous groups of youths left over from football matches. Many of the passengers slept, often sprawled untidily about, the worse for drink. Occasionally he was himself. A visit to the toilet afforded none of the private pleasures of the mornings: the floor was often awash in piss or vomit.

He would read, or sometimes sleep, only rarely speaking to anyone, and then usually only to make a friendly pact with someone sitting opposite for each to wake the other if either were asleep when the train reached Coventry. But there was one group of travellers that interested him, and he felt that he would like to talk to them and be part of them, without knowing why. He had only gradually become aware of the regularity of their habits. They all arrived separately, except for two young women. There was a small, excitable man with a squeaky Cockney voice who seemed to be the life and soul of the party; everyone called him Tony. Then a tall man of about thirty dressed in informal but expensive-looking clothes, with alert, intelligent eyes and a wide humorous mouth. This man had smiled at him once or twice in a resigned fellow-travelling kind of way, when a delay was announced, or when one of the drinkers upset a glass. So he became the Smiler. A dark curly-haired man a little older than the Smiler, who smoked cigars and always arrived just as the train was pulling out. They called him Charles. A short fat Spaniard called Pepe. These seemed to form the core of the group.

It seemed to him that what they had in common was that

they were all heavy drinkers who were well able to handle it. There were no quarrels, nobody became incapable, and if Tony sometimes stumbled on his way down the aisle it was nobody's business but his own. Tony and the two young women drank Tony's gin, the Smiler brought vodka, Charles brought Scotch, and Pepe always arrived with a litre and a half of Soave or Frascati. Mixers, water, beer and snacks were purchased from the buffet, and drinks were shared in a hospitable and indeed rather gracious manner. The whole operation had a style that appealed to him in some obscure way that he did not understand.

One day he bought a half bottle of vodka and carried it round with him in his briefcase until it was time for the late train. He timed his arrival carefully, boarded the train at the first coach after the buffet car, and found the Smiler sitting alone. He sat down, not at the same table but at the one opposite, and smiled at the Smiler, who, to his pleasure and relief, smiled back in a gently encouraging way. Encouraged, he opened his briefcase and took out the vodka.

'D'you fancy, er . . . ?'

'What a good idea,' said the Smiler, smiling more broadly.

'I'm afraid I haven't got any . . .' Dore stood up. 'I'll just go down the, er, and . . .'

'No need,' said the Smiler. 'All here.' He lifted a carrier bag on to his table and produced plastic beakers, lemonade and crisps. 'Come on over.'

It was as easy as that.

And when Tony arrived, he did say, 'Who's your friend, dear?' in a faintly petulant way, but when the Smiler indicated the bottle of vodka Tony cheered up immediately.

'New blood at the bar, always welcome, cheers my dears!'

Over the next few weeks Dore learnt that the little group of friends were simply people who worked in London every day but could not afford to or did not choose to live there. Tony had a tobacco and confectionery shop. The Smiler was a pianist: sessions, theatre orchestras, whatever. Charles was a radio journalist. Pepe was a waiter. The two pretty young women about the same age as his daughters were whores from

Birmingham who took day excursions to London three times a week. They were, of course, by far the highest earners in the group, but they never bought their own drinks. No one seemed to mind about this. Only the Smiler volunteered much information about himself (though never, curiously enough, his name) but they were all ready to talk about each other.

They seemed to him an exceptionally tolerant and amiable group of people; a little secretive and suspicious of outsiders, but once you were acknowledged, you had their full permission to be and do whatever you wanted to be or do. Christine and Paula, for example. They were whores, but within the group this was not something that they were, but simply a job that they did, much like any other job. Like Charles, they had to spend the occasional tedious morning in the Magistrates Court. Like Tony and Pepe they got the occasional stroppy customer. In the train, they were travelling companions, they were friends. They had the group's permission to be whatever they wanted to be. And he had Christine and Paula's permission too, he knew. If only he knew what he wanted.

It was a hot summer. London was almost unbearable. Dore was so glad that he did not live there. One afternoon he found himself catching a Metropolitan Line train from Hammersmith to Euston Square. The morning's meeting had gone exceptionally well and he had, uncharacteristically, had several quick pints in a large cavernous pub opposite the branch office. He was not drunk exactly, but he felt at ease, able to look boldly about him. The train was very dirty and there were graffiti on the insides of the doors, inscribed with bold, shapely fluency but to him totally inscrutable: some kind of territory-marking, probably. More than half the people in the carriage were black.

He was sitting at the end of the carriage in what was almost a little separate compartment; two seats facing another two. Opposite him sat a plump black woman with her thin pretty daughter. He assumed it was a mother and daughter. The girl had a black cotton skirt on that was both thin and short. Her thin dark legs were wonderfully glossy, like polished wood.

155

He raised his eyes and met the eyes of the mother and he smiled, as a father of daughters. The woman looked back coldly for a moment, then turned her head away.

Just as the doors were closing, an elderly chap in a flat cap squeezed through the narrowing opening and half fell into the seat next to him, emitting a loud fruity belch as he did so. He looked a nice, respectable, grandfatherly sort of old codger, but he was distressingly inebriated.

The train pulled out of the station and into the bright sunlight. At first Dore thought the old man was shouting at the top of his voice about Asher and Esher and Pershore; but it was a sneezing fit that rocked his stocky little body forwards and backwards, until his flat cap fell into his lap. He stopped sneezing and stared at the cap through streaming eyes as if he had never seen it before. He was panting, and long shiny streams of mucus hung from his nose and mouth; he seemed at a loss to know what to do about them. Then, as if visited by sudden inspiration, he buried his face in the lining of the cap, blew his nose vigorously, wiped it, and emerged bright-eyed and pink in the face. This presented him with another problem. He stared glumly at the upturned cap for some moments, then like a man steeling himself to do a necessary but unwelcome duty, he pressed the cap firmly back on his bald head.

Dore was experiencing a mixture of feelings: irritation that the old codger had chosen him to sit next to, embarrassment lest he should be asked for assistance or engaged in conversation, or worse, thought to be this dreadful old fart's drinking crony; but also a kind of brotherly concern. The old chap was clearly not a dosser or a down-and-out. He was clean and respectably dressed. He had probably had one or two too many at some old codgers' gathering, poor old fellow. His grandchildren would be distressed to see him in this state. Someone should be looking after him. But it was surely not Dore's responsibility.

The old man groaned noisily and belched again. Dore looked at the black woman opposite but again she would not meet his eye. The thin black girl was staring at the old man in what looked like horrified fascination. Without looking sideways Dore was aware that his neighbour had shifted his position: he felt that he was being looked at. The thin girl's eyes were wide with disbelief. Dore turned his head. The old man, his cap rakishly askew, was staring deeply into his face with every evidence of frank sexual admiration – no, more than that – romantic infatuation. His clear blue boozer's eyes were the eyes of a man who has fallen in love at first sight. Terminally embarrassed, Dore turned his head again, but a few seconds later was aware of something moving behind his shoulders. The old man was slowly, shyly, tentatively, putting his arm around Dore like a bashful teenager on his first date.

For a few seconds Dore ignored it, then realised that that was madness. He had to do something, or the old man would escalate his advances. He turned again to face the old codger, and said in what he hoped was a sharp authoritative tone, but deeply aware of how ridiculous he sounded, 'What's the matter with you?'

'I wouldn't mind a pint of beer,' said the old man coquettishly. 'How'd you like to buy me one?'

'Don't you think you've had enough?' said Dore. God, this was dreadful. He was sounding like some old-fashioned schoolmistress, and worse than that, he was clearly not impressing his authority on his disreputable old admirer at all.

'I'd like to have one with you,' said the old man. 'A whisky if you like. Let's go to your place. We'll have a whisky and a bit of fun.'

Dore stared round wildly. No one would look at him, but he knew they were all listening. He was beginning to panic. He turned to the old man again, determined to be firm.

'Look here,' he said, and then stopped. He didn't know what to say. His face felt painfully hot. He wondered whether he should get out of the train at the next stop, or move to the other end of the coach. But perhaps the old codger was only going a couple of stops himself.

'How far are you going? I mean, what stop do you get off?' As soon as he had spoken he realised that he had said another

157

stupid thing: he had meant to sound offputting and succeeded only in sounding flirtatious.

'I'm getting off where you're getting off,' said the old man roguishly. 'I fancy you, I do. I think you're very tasty. And I think you fancy me as well.'

'Oh, for Christ's sake!' said Dore sharply, at last granted access to a surge of anger strong enough to bring him to his feet, push roughly past the old man, and walk past the awed spectators to the far end of the coach. He found an empty seat and sat there, his face burning, determined not to turn, fearful of being followed; but the old man, perhaps incapable of negotiating the swaying train, stayed where he was, and after a while began sneezing again.

Dore raised his eyes to the face of the woman who sat opposite. She turned her head away sharply. He wanted to say, 'It wasn't *me*. I was the *victim*.' But he was implicated. He was the kind of person to whom that sort of thing is allowed to happen. And through all the irritation, outrage, self-pity, there was something else there, something deeper. After so long in the cold, he was again an object of desire, and he knew himself worthy to be so. The old man, totally arseholed as he was, had not been entirely stupid. His only mistake had been to think of himself as a worthy suitor for Dore's favours. He was not. But he had been able to see what many had not seen: Dore's power to create desire in others. And secure in this knowledge, Dore had only now to wait.

That night he took an early train home, but the following Tuesday he stayed in London late, sat in a cinema, drank in a pub, bought half a bottle of vodka and caught the late train.

Tony was not there; he was said to be on his holidays in Malta. His absence changed things: Dore found himself in a long, rambling, gently exploratory conversation with the Smiler. He learnt to his delight that the Smiler was a father of daughters too: two very pretty little girls aged three and one. He admired their proferred photographs and resolved to bring photographs of his own beautiful grown-up girls next time. He drank more vodka than he meant to, and talked with passionate conviction about the deep satisfaction of being a father of daughters, how the joys increased and multiplied with every year; and the younger man smiled and nodded, happy to be enlightened by a more experienced father of daughters.

Dore was so involved in the conversation that he did not notice the time passing, and he felt quite annoyed when the train pulled into Milton Keynes, which was the Smiler's stop. There was more that Dore wanted to say to the Smiler; he was not sure what it was, but if they had had more time it would come to him. But then he remembered that they had all the time in the world: the late train from Euston departed every night; the weeks, months, years, stretched out ahead of them, docile, ready to be enjoyed. Life was, after all, a kind of feast.

Then something odd happened, something that Dore was to replay over and over in his mind all through the following week. Amongst the passengers coming down the aisle was a pale young man with an angry face, who glared into the face of first one and then another of his fellow-travellers, as if daring them to acts of violence. Warmed and blurred by alcohol, Dore glared back when it was his turn. He was not about to be frightened by this stripling: he was a mature man in the prime of life, and a father of daughters. Moreover, he was strong in the knowledge that he was with friends, he was, for once, on the inside, and no one could intimidate him. No one on this train would intimidate the Smiler either, he was sure, and indeed the Smiler showed no fear. His reaction was, however, far from simple to interpret. He grinned at the angry youth rather mockingly it seemed to Dore, and then he raised his rolled-up newspaper (the *Independent*, Dore could not but notice and remember) and thrust it up and down through the O he made with his left thumb and forefinger. This seemed to Dore an obscurely exotic gesture of contempt, the sort of thing he had only seen in productions of Shakespeare, or television documentaries about undiscovered parts of Spain. But the angry youth, who might himself have been auditioning for a walk-on in *Romeo and Juliet*, seemed to understand, giving the Smiler a curt nod and pushing on towards the end of the carriage.

The Smiler stood up and gave Dore a curiously intimate glance, as if they had something else in common, something deeper even than the kinship shared by the fathers of daughters. Then he glanced towards the disappearing back of the angry youth.

'He looked a bit emotional, didn't you think?' said Dore, wanting to prolong their man-to-man rapport to the last possible moment.

'Yes,' said the Smiler. 'Yes, I thought so. Night, then,' And smiling, he hurried off the train.

'Have a glass of wine, why don't you?' said Pepe, but Dore shook his head. Something had happened, he could feel it. He even knew what it was, somewhere deep inside himself, deeper than the warm clogged feeling in his throat, deeper even than the thumping of his heart. He knew what it was but he was not ready to think about it yet; he was in no hurry to understand it. He had been thrilled by the brief exchange of glances with the angry youth. Dore had not raised his fists in anger since the age of twelve, but he would have been ready to fight, if it had come to a brawl, to fight shoulder to shoulder with his friend the Smiler, two good men and true, two fathers of daughters, teaching the young tearaway a lesson he'd never forget. Yes, he had been stirred enough to want to fight, to whirl his body into furious motion; but now he was calming down. Calming down, but not cooling down. His body felt pleasantly warm. He felt strong and centred. He felt whole. And he knew what it was and that he didn't need to understand it; all he had to do was to enjoy the strong, centred feeling and to wait.

It was a week before he took the late train again. The Smiler was not on board, and Tony was still apparently on his holidays. Charles and Pepe and the two young women made up a four, and Dore found himself on his own again. He read the *Independent* from cover to cover, and when the train slowed down to slide between the quiet, still platforms of Milton Keynes Central and the young man with the angry face came down the aisle and looked him full in the face, Dore was ready. He raised his rolled newspaper and smiled, and the youth looked deep into his eyes and nodded. Dore rose and left the train without a backward glance at his companions.

It was cool in the night air. The young man walked ahead of him along the track towards a little hut by the embankment. Dore could smell cinders and grass and the odour of his own fear and excitement. And it was there, leaning against the creosoted wooden walls of the dark little hut, his hands behind his head, passive and abandoned, his head back staring at the stars, that Dore allowed the fierce youth to search out his yearning prick and set it free, only to plunge it between his warm wet lips. And Dore, a sob catching in his throat and tears on his cheeks, knowing himself to be the worthy object of a passionate desire, felt the identity he had constructed over fifty years dissolve forever as he poured his joyful heart into the stranger's mouth.

Early Bird and Smiley Face

This story could have been about any of the families who stayed that year in English Alley at the Grande Métairie. The Grande Métairie is a four-star campsite in Brittany and we found ourselves in English Alley because we had booked with the same English company. We lived in tents like little houses with two bedrooms, a living room and a kitchen, a place to put the car, and a little square of garden at the back. The sun shone throughout the fortnight and the air was full of Ambre Solaire, coconut oil, Savlon, TCP, and the patient desperation of the English families.

It could have been about any of them: Topless, The Prat, In the Trade, Fatty Peugeot, or even one of the grey families without faces who disappeared all day and zipped their tent flaps early at night. There was desperation there, too, in the obsessively hammered tent-pegs, the neat stacks of Beanos and Word Search books, the sad backs I stood behind while waiting for my turn to shave. Fatty Peugeot was fat and spent his days talking about the excellence of his Peugeot, though he never drove his family to the beach in it. In the Trade was in the trade; Nadine and Sharon dirtied different frilly dresses every day and had their legs smacked for it every evening. The Prat was a prat. He had a jolly red face and baggy shorts, and what he liked best was to hold his children upside down and shake them until their faces went purple and their francs showered into the dust. He thought that they enjoyed this as much as he did. Topless was called Topless because of his interest in topless beaches. He was a tall, fair, good-looking fellow with a slight, pretty wife and two slight, pretty little girls. This was the year that Brittany began to go topless, and every day Topless dragged his family off to ever more remote

165

and topless beaches on the Côte Sauvage, beaches you had to scramble down cliffs to; and every evening they returned, the wife wan and weary, the little girls tetchy with skinned knees from the cliff-scrambling, Topless grinning and prancy but with an unsatisfied glitter in his light blue eyes, as if yet more topless beaches lurked in the shimmering distance beyond the jagged rocks. Yes, it could well have been about Topless.

It couldn't have been about us, of course. We are good at being a family. We nurse each other through with tolerance and shared jokes. We pick our own mussels off the beach and cook them in *Gros Plant*, but we're not doctrinaire about it. We have our books to retreat into. We have irony. We have detachment. You have to take my word for this because I, after all, am telling this story. You have to look at things from our tent. You'll be all right there. Promise.

No, it's about Early Bird and Smiley Face, three tents along from us on the same side of English Alley. Early Bird was called Early Bird because she always got up so early, and Smiley Face was called Smiley Face because he never smiled. My daughter made these names for them on the first day, before we knew their real names, but when we knew their real names we found it hard to remember them. I am glad that Lisa named them so quickly and so surely. I think it helped later – a bit.

The first thing Early Bird did every morning was to put on her false eyelashes. She never seemed to wear any other make-up. Indeed, she was something of a scruff, with untidy dark curly hair, pale skin, cotton nightie tucked into blue jeans, bare feet with long dirty toes. She had a mouth which changed shape all the time, even when she wasn't talking, which she was, most of the time. Rather a beauty, in her way. I thought so. I liked to watch her in the mornings, throwing heaps of dirty clothes out of the tent, squatting on her heels in the dust to play five-stones with her children, pattering up and down the rows of tents with her pale dirty feet. She made it all seem a bit of a game. I thought so.

Smiley Face was not usually sighted before eleven, though he could be heard for an hour before that, snapping and growling at his children, trying to drive them out of the tent. Then he would emerge himself, a stocky, olive-skinned, scowling man with a neat brown moustache. He would set up a metal table on his little square of back garden, place a metal chair by its side, fetch a bottle of red wine and a glass, and start the day's drinking. 'Unhurriedly, with a kind of controlled anger, Smiley Face begins the day's long punishment of the *Caves Cooperatives*.' (From the notes I made at the time. I must have seen him as material even then. 'Kind of controlled anger'. I ask you.)

On the third morning Early Bird came to call. We were sitting having breakfast on the dusty patch at the front of our tent that we called the patio.

'Have you enrolled them in the Club Micky?' she said.

'Who?' my wife asked. Tom and Lisa looked up warily.

'The children. It's absolutely the answer. Activities all day, they learn French, it's really good value. Then you can . . .', she waved a pale thin arm in a way that suggested infinite possibilities . . . 'hang loose. Whatever! Gosh, boiled eggs, you *are* organised!' She squatted on her heels in the dust and took a bite out of Lisa's banana. 'Mm, lovely! Well, what about this Club Mickey, then? Ours adore it, honestly!'

We have always been better than average at refusing the hard sell, but there was something difficult to resist about Early Bird, and something flattering about the way she had chosen us out of all the families in English Alley. After breakfast we crammed both sets of children into the car (Smiley Face, it was understood, would neither drive his car in the morning nor surrender his keys) and drove down the bumpy track to the beach.

Early Bird and Smiley Face had three children: James, in shock from his first term at boarding school, his gentle face numb and tense with the effort to get things right. And Chloe and Ruth, wild little scruffs like their mother.

'Feet out the window, everybody!' yelled Ruth forcefully, and

Early Bird and her daughters thrust their pale feet and dirty toes out of the windows, while James sat with his fists clenched between his knees, catatonic with embarrassment.

'You are wet, James,' said Chloe.
 'Man put his feet out the window!' shouted Ruth.
 'Man's driving, darling,' said Early Bird.

The Club Micky was a miniature concentration camp on the beach. Inside the wire fence were swings and rings and a trampoline and a hut. It cost rather more than twice what I had thought possible, and it looked exactly the sort of place where French kids could gang up on English kids and make them desperate and miserable, while the swarthy French louts who supervised would lurk in their cool dank hut exploring each other's hangups, or even bodies. I felt the accusation in Tom's and Lisa's eyes but I avoided looking at them.

On the way back Early Bird stuck only one of her feet out of the window. 'This is really awfully nice of you,' she said.
 'My pleasure,' I said, which is what I always say, because it takes too long to explain, and people don't want to know about the exact proportions of pleasure, irritation, resentment, amusement, anger, guilt and despair I experience in doing things for them. You don't, do you? ('Thanks for writing me this story.' 'My pleasure. Thanks for reading it.')

'That's frightfully suave of you,' she said, indicating that perhaps she did understand, and then, alarmingly, 'You're a very appealing sort of chap, aren't you?'
 I concentrated on driving between the pot-holes, keenly aware that the leg that was not out of the window was resting against mine.
 'Never mind,' she said. 'It's a shitty old world, isn't it?' She made that seem a bit of a game too.
 'Look,' she said as we turned into English Alley, 'D'you mind awfully if I sort of come and dump on you and your wife for a little while? I don't really want to go back to the tent, and I can't get off the camp because he won't give me the keys.'

'Feel free,' I said, which is another thing I say. 'We're not doing anything special.'

So for an hour or two we sat on our dusty patio while Early Bird told us all about herself and Smiley Face: how she had married him straight from school and what a desperate mistake it had been. She hadn't known anything then except that she liked chaps to be handsome and brown and sexy, all of which Smiley Face had been when she first met him; and full of brooding intensity, which seemed to be absolutely the thing except that what he was brooding intensely about, even then, was probably how to avoid spending money on anyone else while contriving to have a bloody good time himself. This Brittany holiday was a particular case in point, because somehow Early Bird had forgotten to bring her own francs with her, and Smiley Face was punishing her by refusing to eat out in restaurants, and insisting on two hot meals a day, three courses each, cooked by Early Bird on a rickety Calor Gas burner. It was a miserable story, but she made it entertaining, even exhilarating.

He's the most terrible man in the world,' she said proudly. 'An absolute ... bounder.' Her eyes sparkled. 'Look at him!' We looked down English Alley. There he sat, alone at his table, well down his second bottle of red wine. Early Bird waved. Smiley Face glowered. 'Absolute bounder.'

Then my wife and I went to fetch the kids back from the Club Micky. When we got to the beach it looked like a deserted battlefield: broken toys, torn comics. Ruth and Lisa were sitting by the fence, their faces streaked with tears. James sat on the sand a little further off, pretending to read a tattered French comic. We asked them where Tom and Chloe had gone.

'Escaped,' said Lisa. 'They're down by the sea.'
'Why didn't you escape?'
'We were too small and James was too wet.'
'What was the trouble?'
'French kids ganged up on us.'
'What were the ... supervisors doing?'

'Dunno. They stayed in the hut.'

'It's all right,' said my wife. 'You don't have to go any more.'

'We'll have to,' said James. 'Because Daddy paid for the week.'

The sullen louts in the hut took our strictures philosophically but refused to tip up any refunds. I admired the style of the girl, who communicated a powerful contempt and apathy with the minimum of shrug and monosyllable. At one point she sighed and raised her arms slowly to put her hands behind her head. The hair in her armpits was long, tangled and sweaty. There was a smell in the hut: cool, seaweedy. Snatched, gritty, late-adolescent sex. Nobody put their feet out of the window on the way back to English Alley.

Holidays with us often begin as a series of baffling false starts. But we are good at being a family: we ride the false starts and wait for the pattern. The pattern that emerged was long days on the Côte Sauvage beaches, later and later meals, more and more *Gros Plant*, less and less thought. By the end of the first week I had abandoned *Vanity Fair* and felt better for it. Often we took Early Bird's children with us, sometimes Early Bird herself. Her children found our absent-minded tolerance comforting. We found her dramas stimulating. She told us more about herself and Smiley Face, often featuring her own contribution to 'our little disaster on wheels': extravagance, domestic incompetence, her flings and her breakouts.

'He can't control me, you see,' she would say, shaking the water out of her curly hair so that it ran down the Speedo one-piece she looked fourteen in. 'He'd love to control me, but he can't. Hopeless! Disaster! What's next? Frisbee?'

Often Chloe, who had fallen in love with us, would come and sleep in our tent. She had to sleep with a night light, she wet the bed and she had nightmares. None of us seemed to mind this too much.

And English Alley continued to be English Alley, its residents continuing to perform pleasingly in the characters we had written for them. Nadine In The Trade said the camp swimming pool was rubbish and then fell in it. In the Trade, who shared her opinion, smacked her legs for it just the same. The Prat chortled up and down; we longed for his children to up-end him, but they never did. One evening Topless came home red-faced and aggrieved; he had been arrested and questioned for being bottomless on a topless beach. I thought I detected a sly *Schadenfreude* on his wife's pretty face, but I couldn't be sure.

The day after that I was lying in the tent after lunch. My wife had taken the children for the obligatory visit to the menhirs, a mile or so away. I wanted to be the only man who had been to Carnac and never seen a menhir. I had reached that pleasant state where I no longer needed to read, think, talk, smoke or drink. I was lying on the air-bed naked, and if I was thinking about anything, it was that my legs were satisfactorily brown right up to the crotch, browner even than my naturally swarthy cock, which was at the time flopped indolently across the narrow strip of white belly my bathers covered on the beach. The tent flap opened and Early Bird came in, blinking from the sunshine.

'Hello,' she said, and then, 'oh, sorry. Are you busy?'

'No, no. Um . . . feel free,' I said.

It's useful isn't it, to have things that you always say.

She squatted on her heels beside me and took my cock in her hand. 'That's a nice one,' she said.

We watched it grow in her hand for a little while, like a couple of patient gardeners. Then she let it go and smiled at me as if this too was all a bit of a game.

'Some people say that's absolutely the solution,' she said. 'But I think it's probably just part of the problem. Actually, what I came to say was, Richard wondered if you'd like to come over for a drink with him.'

For a moment I wondered who Richard was, and then I remembered that Richard was Smiley Face's name.

'My pleasure,' I said.

'I'm sorry, Joe,' she said. 'I mean, if we were in Wolverhampton or something . . . shitty world. Never mind.' She leaned over and kissed me on the nose. The touch of her lips was dry and feathery.

Smiley Face was sitting in his usual place at the table, wearing his usual blue shorts. He was very brown, and close to his body looked even more solid. Thick and smooth without being fat. Like a shark's body. He nodded to me and I sat on the stool opposite him. There was an open bottle of red wine on the table and four more in the shade underneath.

'Don't worry,' said Smiley Face. 'There's plenty more in the tent.' And we began to drink.

'This is a damned unsatisfactory holiday,' said Smiley Face halfway down the first bottle. I said that I was sorry to hear this, and he went on to explain that the camp was not satisfactory from the women's point of view, that the cooking facilities were totally inadequate. No wonder the women were miserable and bolshy.

'Is your wife miserable and bolshy?' he asked.

'Not really,' I said, and then, to excuse myself, 'we haven't been doing much cooking, and what we do, we tend to share.'

'You don't believe in the division of labour?'

'Not really, no,' I said, wishing I could sound a bit less apologetic about it.

'Well, I'm sure you won't mind my telling you you're making a bloody big mistake,' said Smiley Face. He was speaking in a quiet conversational tone but his eyes were glaring into mine with uncomfortable intimacy. He filled my glass.

'Of course, Marianne's unstable,' he said. Again for a moment I wondered who he was talking about.

'She's . . . volatile,' I offered carefully.

'Volatile? She's unbalanced. Look at the bloody children. They're all unbalanced.'

'We like them,' I said. I was going to say more, but he stared at me with what looked like such hatred that I stopped. I was beginning to realise how hot the sun was in that little square of garden, bouncing back almost tangibly off the metal table top. I drank some more wine and Smiley Face filled my glass immediately.

'What d'you think of this stuff?' he said.

'Fine.'

'But will it travel? That's what I'm trying to find out. How the hell can you tell?' There was something splendid about Smiley Face's anger. It embraced the whole material world.

We drank some more wine, and the heat of the sun became easier to deal with. After the second bottle, Smiley Face's anger seemed to ease off, and he started to tell me a long rambling story about a holiday he had enjoyed, perhaps the only holiday he had enjoyed, before his marriage. He had been here in Brittany, camping with a group of friends, all male. Swimming, he said, fishing, water-skiing, diving off rocks. Primitive camping in two-man tents. I imagined them together with their hard, round bodies, seven or eight of them on a rock with water dripping off their dark moustaches, flopping lazily one by one into the blue water, swimming slowly in a long line towards the misty horizon; the reluctance with which they would turn, snorting like walruses, and swim slowly back to the clutter and complication of the shore.

When I started to pay attention again he was talking about Ireland. I misunderstood him, thought he was still talking about holidays, and he stood up angrily and stumped off to his tent. When he came back he was carrying two more bottles of red wine, which he placed carefully under the table, and something wrapped in cloth that he put on the table between us. He unwrapped the cloth. It was a revolver.

'Go ahead,' he said. 'Pick it up.'

I picked it up. I know nothing about guns at all. This one looked big and clumsy and felt extraordinarily heavy in my hand. It hurt my wrist to hold it. It frightened me.

'Chap I knew in Ireland,' said Smiley Face, 'actually he was a good friend of mine, shot himself with this. Made a dog's breakfast of it. Blew the side of his face off. He couldn't even get that right. You know, I couldn't forgive him for that.'

In the sort of fiction I usually write, the kind I make such a good living at, you don't bring a gun into a story without eventually firing it. People feel cheated, don't they? So, possibilities: Smiley Face shoots himself. Smiley Face shoots Early Bird. And/or his children. Early Bird shoots Smiley Face. And so on. Or something ironic and oblique; we could foreground Fatty Peugeot and give him a flesh wound. *We* won't get shot. We have to be there for the end of the story. But there's the gun on the table. We've put it there now. You could say the same about a cock, of course. Or a pen. Or Fatty Peugeot. Nothing is for nothing. But we're trying to do something different in this story, aren't we? We're trying to say what it's really like. Do you mind me talking to you like this?

The thing about Marianne,' said Smiley Face after a bit. 'I can't bear her, and I can't let her go. That's the thing. And I'll tell you something else. I've felt like this about everything I've cared for.'

The sun seemed to have got hotter again. I wanted to speak to Smiley Face but my tongue felt huge, dry and swollen. I tried to focus on his face. Sweat was running in streams down his hard brown forehead, glistening in his eyebrows. One of his eyes looked much smaller than the other one. I realised that I was very drunk indeed and in need of some kind of help. I managed to say something about this.

'Sun on your head,' said Smiley Face. 'Bad for you. Get under the table. Cooler there.'

I recognised that there was something bizarre about this suggestion and tried to say something about getting back to the tent.

'No,' said Smiley Face. 'Get under the fucking table. It's all you're fucking good for.'

I realised that it was very important indeed to get up and walk back to our tent and lie down. I put my hands on the table and pushed myself up. The stool fell over but I was on my feet. I turned and walked back towards the tent. I heard a small metallic sound behind me but I didn't turn round. I had some confused notion about officers and gentlemen not shooting people in the back.

I fell on the bed and dreamed about Smiley Face, half his head gone, pursuing me through a restaurant which was also a cliffside. Somewhere in the dream I was Smiley Face as well, and I woke to a moment of authentic terror, having no idea not only where I was but who I was. Chloe and Lisa were looking at me with great interest.

'You were shouting really loud,' said Lisa. 'Everyone was coming to listen.'

I tried to explain to my wife about Smiley Face but I was still incoherent and she was not sympathetic. She told the girls to take me for a walk to get rid of me and sober me up.

'Where shall we take him?' said Chloe.

'I don't care. Take him to the menhirs.'

This seemed a terrible idea to me, but I was too weak to resist. The two little girls took me, one to each arm, and dragged me jabbering and stumbling along the path the camp ponies used. I was aware of people staring, standing back, pressing against the fence. Then I noticed that there were no more people and we had reached the menhirs.

The sun was going down. We were almost the only people there. Us and the menhirs. The girls led me down the whole length of the site. I had had no idea there were so many of them: blank, smooth, people-sized lumps of flat stone, standing in little groups, like silent families. So many of them, and no reason for them, blank, silent, grey, pointless. Who had decided when to stop? Who had decided that it was finished, that there were enough families?

By the time we got back to the other camp, our camp, I was making more sense and walking unsupported. I went and had a shower, and not much later gave a tolerable imitation of a family man eating *côte d'agneau grillé au feu de bois* in one of the places where this was all too easy to do. Though my wife insisted on driving both ways. When we got back to English Alley it was quite dark, and I was slowly being forgiven. The afternoon was being gradually processed into anecdote, like the Topless Bottomless story.

'He was groaning really loud all the way there, and he walked right through a great pile of horseshit!'

'Dad, did Smiley Face really try to make you get under the table?'

We were good at being a family. We knew how to handle these things.

Before I went to bed I went and stood in the dark on our little dust patio. It was quiet in English Alley. The zips were closed. Only Topless's tent showed a flickering light behind the canvas, Topless presumably scanning his detailed maps for that elusive and ultimately topless beach. In the Trade's vast estate car sat quietly in the moonlight like a patient hearse.

Then, without meaning to, I glanced over to Smiley Face's garden. He was still sitting alone at the table, alone in the dark. I felt frightened, knowing that something dreadful and final was going to happen, knowing too that I was part of it, and that I should go over, and try to avert it, or take my part in it. But I didn't. I went back in our tent where it was safe.

I had a different dream that night. I dreamt that the sea had come up and engulfed the camp: bits of tent, jumbled clothes, cardboard boxes leaking food were eddying about in the filthy water, full of drowned families. I was looking for my family but I couldn't find them, because all the cars were the same, and when I peered inside them the families had no faces, no distinguishing characteristics. They were all blank and smooth and flat, four or five to a car, grey and rounded and blank, like the menhirs.

I woke late, my head throbbing, and remembered. After a little while I was able to go out and look down the alley towards Smiley Face and Early Bird's tent. It was empty, and a couple of jolly young reps in red T-shirts were spring-cleaning it, shaking out the airbeds and putting empty bottles in sacks. Early Bird and Smiley Face had gone.

I am writing this at night, on the verandah of our villa in Corfu. We have more money now, but we are not so good at being a family. Below me the sea beats regularly, and there are more stars in the sky than I can be doing with. Inside the villa my wife is in bed in one bedroom, Lisa and her friend are in bed in the other bedroom. Tom won't come away with us any more. It is very late, but I don't want to go in. I want to sit out here on my own and think about Early Bird and Smiley Face. I can't bear all this, but I can't let it go. My pen lies on the table.

Into Europe: Two. Some Aspects of the Economy

1. Getting Into The Economy

In the Economy is where they are and consequently that is where you have to be to get in. On the kaserns it's mostly young guys and career soldiers who are married to the Army. In the economy we have enlisted men E2s and above, they apply to get a rent allowance and that is called living in the economy. That is where they live and that is where we hit them. Many of them are married with young families. The Army was their way out of the shit. Now they want more for their kids than they had. They are buying the Future.

Learn your script. It may sound like bullshit to you clever guys and girls but it has worked before and it will work again, it has been honed smooth and solid by the blood and tears and brains of better men than you, believe me.

How you get in the apartment block is up to you. They have pretty good security but there are ways. Stroll along just as the guy exercising his dog gets back to base. Hi there, fella, let him sniff you, give him a pat and a shake, fine dog you have there, sir, and you are *in*. Or maybe it's a lady struggling to get a baby carriage out through one of the security doors, let me help you with that, ma'am, and you are *in*. There are many ways. The basement garage has automatic doors, so stand in the shadow of the doors. A car comes along, the door opens, you walk in smoothly behind the car before it shuts again and you are *in*. When you are in, walk straight to the elevator, no hesitation, look like a guy that lives in the economy, go straight to the top and work down. Getting in the apartment block is easy. If you want to get in bad enough you will get in. And you want to get in bad enough. If you don't get in you don't eat. So getting in the economy is the least of your worries.

2. Getting in The Apartment

Read the name on the door, that and your script is all you have to deal with. Let's say it's Mr and Mrs Herbert Haggerty. Now forget everything you heard from any other sales organisation, you crowd up real close on the door. As she opens it, step back but not before. Step back and *smile*. Let's say it's the wife and she's got a kid like so high clinging to her leg, OK?

This is you: Hi, Mrs Haggerty, is Herb at home right now? She goes, no he ain't, and she's about to shut the door, but you keep right on smiling and talking. I'm Paul from London, London, England, like that's the only place in England they've ever heard of, I'm your AFL representative here in Bamberg, Herb was sure keen to – then you leave it, squat down, talk to the kid: Hi fella, how you making out? And she's going, AFL, now what is that? And you go, don't you worry, Mrs Haggerty, I got two of these at home I know this one must keep you busy, I won't keep you any longer, tell Herb I called like he said and I'll try to get back to him, and then you stand up and smile again, like you're going to turn away, and she says, AFL what *is* this and then like you suddenly thought of it you say, well maybe I *could* talk to you Mrs Haggerty, I mean it's nothing top secret or anything. Then you *look down at the mat*. Don't ask me why you do that. Just look down at the mat, look up and smile. She will step back two paces, you keep on coming, smiling and talking, and you are *in the apartment*.

3. In The Apartment: an Ideal Scenario

The apartment is clean and tidy. Bob is an E3 and his face is full of the future. Linda is his pretty young wife. Two little kids are playing quietly in the corner. You can even see two or three books. This is a Black family. That is good. Blacks and other ethnics represent your best bet. Let's say we have got through the preliminaries and you are making your pitch.

YOU

You see, Bob, what American Futures offers you is a complete educational and counselling service for the young American family, right through those crucial formative years when your children's future is being determined.

BOB

Hell, though, my kids go to nursery school, they're doing fine, ain't that what schools are for?

YOU

Why sure, Bob, and American Futures give a very good rating to the fine schools here in Bamberg. But if you could give your children that much more, if you could give them personalised, individual counselling, the kind that sets a kid right on course for college, professions like law and medicine . . . if you could give them all that, Linda, for *less than a dollar a week*, well I guess that's an offer I couldn't turn down . . . could you?

LINDA

Well, geez, I dunno, Paul, like this is just a two-year tour for Bob . . . I guess maybe we'll leave it till we're back in the States, what do you say, Bob?

BOB

Yeah, honey, I guess that'd be –

YOU

Linda, Bob, I'm glad you said that because there is a very good reason why you should join now. You're out here doing a good job for America, and American Futures wants to do something especially for you, and all the young American military families here in Europe. As an incentive for you to enrol tonight, the League has authorised me to ship to you a *complete home reference library* at no cost to you whatsoever.

Lean across the table, look deep into their faces. First the husband, then the wife.

YOU

> I guess it's our way of . . . well, hell, excuse me, ma'am. You're out here defending freedom's frontiers. And we want you to know that, well, America appreciates that.

By now the tears should be rolling down their fucking faces as you open the case and spill the shit all over the carpet.

Inside the Apartment (2) Four Case Studies

2) The apartment door is open which is very unusual. I knock on it and this voice yells 'What?' and I say I'm Paul, your AFL representative here in Bamberg, and the guy says to come on through. The hall is kind of messy and still no sign of the guy, Sergeant Damon Bullwinkel of the First and Forty-Fifth, 'If It Flies It Dies'. No sign of Mrs Bullwinkel or any little Bullwinkels either. When I get in the living room I see why Damon didn't come to the door. He is sitting on the couch with a twelve-pack in white boxer shorts and a vest that doesn't quite cover his big pale hairy belly, and his right leg is in plaster from the ankle to the groin. He is drinking the beer out of an orange plastic Tupperware type beaker. Clearly a fastidious man with discrimination and terrific taste. He asks me if I want a beer and I say yes, I'll gladly have a beer with him. Kevin told us that: always say yes, and don't just say yes, say it in a way that makes a bond between you. He tells me where I can find the other beaker and I go in the kitchen and get it, and pour myself a beer, and make the pitch to Damon.

I handle the volumes very tenderly, stroking the covers and the spines with my fingertips. I have become an expert in book massage. My demo set falls open naturally at the illustration depicting the differences between the sexes in childhood, at puberty and in maturity, in terms of primary and secondary sexual characteristics. I don't allude to this at all in my pitch, but I can see that Damon is taking an interest.

184

His own secondary sexual characteristics are pretty impressive. In fact he owns what in another context I might describe as a fabulous pair of knockers. What a strange world it is, to be sure. Why am I here with my broken heart, thousands of miles from home, trying to sell a second-rate children's encyclopaedia to a twenty-two stone US Army sergeant with a broken leg and a bust like a nursing mother?

I can think these thoughts quite freely because I have committed my script to memory and I can reel it out at will: I am telling Damon that this is what he is getting absolutely free of charge; this twenty-volume set, luxury bound in scarlet LeatherTex; and I hold it out so that he can too stroke the spine and caress the pages with his sticky fingers. Feel free, Damon, I tell him, because both cover and pages are guaranteed wash proof, damp proof and scratchproof, and that is ten thousand pages, Damon, twelve hundred illustrations . . .

I notice that Damon is fumbling in his boxer shorts and I find myself hesitating as he pulls out his small, plump, rather doughy-looking penis and contemplates it with pursed lips.
  'You go ahead, boy' he tells me. 'Don't pay no mind to me.'

It's far from easy to follow these instructions. I find myself watching entranced as Damon drains his orange plastic beaker, belches and then, frowning, holds it under the pale flower of his manhood.

I inform him that his Complete Home Reference Library contains no less than six million words, each one of them written by an established expert in his field. Damon pisses copiously into the beaker; it's a high ringing sound, quite brisk and cheerful. I invite him to notice how, no matter which way I turn the pages to the light, there is no reflection or glare, because the paper has been specially selected and subjected to a new scientific process . . .
  Damon has filled his beaker to the brim. He sets it down carefully on the table. He takes another can and pulls the tab off. He seems to pour it into the beaker, and then he stops and frowns. He has a problem. I have a problem too. I have

forgotten the lines of my script. We sit there staring at each other for quite a long while.

b) I am in another apartment making a pitch to this not very happy American family. The wife is pale and thin and she looks tense and frightened. She is sitting on the couch twisting her hands round and round each other. The husband stands in the middle of the room in his vest and trousers. He is holding a bedsheet which is stained with shit. The child, a boy of about seven, is standing on the coffee table, where his father has just placed him. He is wearing a pyjama top and his face is bruised. I am not making very good progress with the pitch, because everything I say to this man seems to fuel his anger. I am thinking that if I can make a sale here it will be a real feather in my cap.

'You telling me you could make something out of an animal like *this*? You want to see an example of this animal's homework?' He shakes the shitty sheet at me. 'Here is an example of this animal's homework!'

The kid is shaking. The woman is looking down at her hands.

'Are you trying to tell me this animal has a *future*?'

I am shaking a little myself, but I tell the angry man that yes, sure his son has a future, and that childhood goes through phases, and that the child guidance program we at American Futures are offering can help in just such tricky periods of development as this. Here is a great opportunity for us to look together at the way an individualised learning program would work for his son. I smile at the kid and ask him what his name is, but he is too traumatised to speak.

The woman looks up.

'He's called . . .'

The man turns and yells at her.

'*Shut up!* Let the animal speak!'

He turns back to the kid. 'You heard the man. Tell him your name!'

The kid can't speak.

'Tell him your fucking name, animal!'

186

He seems about to hit the kid. I hear someone shouting, and it is me.

'Don't hit the kid!'

The angry man turns and stares at me, his fists clenched. *'What?'*

Now I can hardly speak. It comes out as a whisper.

'Don't hit the kid, please. Please don't hit him.'

c) A cold night and I have had a long wait to get into the economy tonight. Standing in the shadow of the automatic garage doors with a black Moroccan guy selling watches and portable telephones. I could feel him staring at me and when I looked at him he gave me this kind of brotherly salute – I guess we are all niggers now. Finally a car comes through and I walk smoothly through behind it before the door closes, and go up to the top floor. I have not tried this building before. Things have not been so good since the cold weather started and I have not eaten for two days. When I am alone and walking the dark streets after a night's work I sometimes burst into tears without warning. And when I am waiting outside an apartment door I find that I am mouthing the words of my script. The name on this door is Sergeant Lasky. I am mouthing to myself: Hi, Sergeant Lasky, I'm Paul, Paul from London England, I'm your AFL representative here in Bamberg . . .

The door opens and there is an unshaven man in his vest and undershorts with a very strange look on his face. I get as far as telling him that my name is Paul and then I nearly faint as I see that he has pulled a gun on me.

'Inside,' he says. 'Inside, calm and slow.'

'Listen,' I say, 'I'm not trying to . . .'

'Inside, asshole!' He sticks the gun into my stomach, and he tells me to put my hands up and walk straight ahead of me. I go down the corridor and into the living room, and I'm trying to explain I'm only the AFL rep, but he shoves me up against the wall and spreads my legs and searches me for weapons. Then again. I am trying to stop shaking.

'So where do you keep it?' yells Lasky in my ear. 'Where's your piece, man?'

'I'm not armed,' I tell him. 'Please let me go.'

'You must be fucking crazy, man' he says. 'This is a fucking war zone, and you're not fucking carrying? Turn around, man, open the valise.'

My nose is bleeding and I have made a stain on the wall. I hope he had not noticed this. I turn around and open the case. My hands are shaking so much that I can hardly work the clasps. Sergeant Lasky stares at the Complete Home Reference Library.

'So what is this shit?'

'Just, just books,' I tell him. 'I sell encyclopaedias. Oh, Christ.' My voice sounds like a little kid's and I am crying now. He stares at me, baffled, furious.

'What did you say your name was?'

'Paul. Paul Green.'

He sucks in air through his teeth.

'I dunno,' he says. 'I think I ought to blow you away, Paul. You understand this is nothing personal, I'm just trying to stay alive.'

I try to tell him that I represent no threat to him but he sticks the gun in my neck.

'You think I'm crazy? I'm not crazy. I'm a soldier, man. You know what that's like? I'll tell you what it's like. People try to kill me everywhere I fucking go, man, do you understand what I am saying here?'

I manage to tell him that I do understand, but that I am on his side, I am with American Futures. This seems to help a little. He takes the gun away from my throat and peers into my eyes.

'What you say your name was?'

'Paul.'

'And you're on my side?'

'Yes, I am.'

'You been in combat, Paul?'

'No, I haven't. Not yet.'

'I been in combat. You ever killed a guy, Paul?'

'No.' My voice has seized up again. He puts his hand on my shoulder, almost affectionately.

'Don't pay no attention to what they say,' he says. 'It ain't so hard to handle. What you say your name was?'

'Paul.'

'I want to give you something, Paul. Wait there.'

He points his finger at me, then turns and goes into the bedroom. I bend over and click the case shut. I am trying to calculate my chances of getting to the apartment door. But my legs feel too weak to run.

Lasky comes back. He is carrying something small and bright. A cap badge.

'This is for your, Paul,' he says. 'You're one of the good guys. This was with me in Nam. Wear it with pride.'

'Thank you, Sergeant Lasky,' I say. 'I certainly will. Thanks a lot. It's been good to talk to you.' I pick the case up and start walking slowly towards the door.

'Yeah,' he says.

I am nearly at the door. I have my hand on the handle when he says, 'Hey, Paul.'

I turn around.

'I came that close to blowing you away, man!'

He is laughing.

d) Milton McCloud's apartment is maybe the shabbiest I have seen on the economy. Everything looks worn, temporary, makeshift. But he does have a TV and a video, and a pornographic video is flickering quietly away now. A little girl of about five in a thin cotton dress and bare feet sits quietly watching the film. It is as if Milton McCloud has recreated a Deep South rural slum in the Federal Republic of West Germany.

Milton McCloud himself is a huge, sad, black man. He sits on the couch, hunched over himself, and his voice is low and slow. Somehow I can't seem to get started on the pitch. I ask Milton how he is liking it here in Bamberg, and he says not so good. I tell him I'm really sorry to hear that and I ask him what the trouble is. He says he guesses I know what his trouble is: he can't pay me. He would like to pay me, but he can't, because he hasn't got the money, and that's the whole truth of it. Clearly he has mistaken me for someone else. I ask him what his talking about.

'You know what I'm talking about, man' he says. 'American Futures. Now don't get me wrong. I ain't blaming no one but myself, Paul. Maybe Sheila came on a little strong, but I signed the paper, and that's how I got myself into a world of trouble. Yes, sir.'

Now I understand.

'You couldn't meet the payments.'

'That is it. Yes, sir. I couldn't meet those payments.'

The little girl turns and smiles at me, then looks back at the screen.

'You know I never looked in any of those books, Paul. I told them that, I asked them would they take the books back, they all still in the boxes, excepting the Bible there. They say no, these books are mine now, they want the money. Which I ain't got. They know you been writing to the Commandant, about how I am a delinquent debtor, and I am in bad there too. Yes, sir. I am suspended from duties, awaiting dishonourable discharge. You know I never been in trouble before, I used to love the army. Well I guess that's the way things turn out sometimes.'

He turns to the little girl and says, almost absentmindedly: 'Put your legs down, honey, straighten your dress.'

The little girl does as he tells her. In the film, people are silently fucking, their heaving pink bodies filling the screen. I try to think of something to say to Milton McCloud.

'Shit. That's awful. I'm so sorry, Milton.'

It doesn't sound too good, does it? Milton is twice my size. Why doesn't he pick me up and throw me into the street? But he turns and manages a smile, as if it is his duty to comfort me. 'Hey,' he says. 'It ain't nothing for your to worry about. No one blames you. I understand you have your work to do.'

* * *

The beggars squat in the middle of the town, outside the elegant small boutiques. The beggars are more neatly turned out and more efficient than English beggars. None of them have bottles, and all of them have small cardboard placards which they hold in their hands or prop against the wall beside them. These placards look very well cared for, and the information on them is neatly laid out, impeccably lettered, and correctly spelt. The most informative is propped up next to a rather scholarly-looking middle-aged woman, and sets out a complete table of her weekly expenses, and how much she needs to beg in a day to stay alive.

The simplest is in the hands of a tall thin, red-haired man in his twenties. This one says simply '*Ich bin in Not. Wer will hilfen?*' It says he is in need and asks who will help. The answer to that one is: a few people will, but not very many. If he were a few years younger, or forty years older, he would do better.

This is Rust's idea for the end of the movie: after our hero has been traumatised by the pain and despair in the economy, after his ideological and emotional bankruptcy has been unpacked by the skinny but sexy, left-wing, contemptuous German bint, after his love had been first accepted but then relinquished by the black American girl soldier from the deep South, after he has understood that the speaking of too many lies can make a man mute, we find him in the final frames sitting on the pavement in the middle of the comfortable, prosperous, South German shopping mall, holding a notice which says: '*Ich bin in Not. Wer will hilfen?*'

For Rust, that says it all, and also expresses a few things that he has been feeling while blundering round these smug and beautiful Bavarian townships. The American money, it need hardly be said, doesn't agree. The American money sees that ending as perversely downbeat and cynical. The Germans aren't keen either. They get together with the British producer and reach a swift agreement that Rust isn't giving them what they want. Then they screw Rust in two or three of the ways available to them and get another writer in. Not long after that the Berlin Wall comes down and Europe is a whole different ball game. It is quite clear that the entire project will have to be aborted.

But those half-formed wants, those unexpressed desires that wheel like bats and moths out in the clear cold Bavarian darkness and flop occasionally against the lighted windows! That terrible father, locked into his cycle of rage and release; that little boy, condemned now forever to screw up his face and wince in expectation of the certain blow. Lasky, poor crazy Lasky, stuck in his nightmare of a Nam he is surely too young to have even seen combat in. How shall he be freed? Will Damon drink and piss, plastered for eternity? How long must Milton McCloud be bent over by the weight of his debts? And Paul, our AFL representative in the economy? He's fading. Look. You can see right through him to the pavement.

If they aren't given their lives to live, how can they get better? They're just the same as us. Everybody wants to be in the movie. Even Rust.

Well, I've laid claim to my territory. I'm lucky. I'm in a prime position. You can see me any day, just outside the bakers, where the warm air comes up/through the grating. You can try to meet my eye but I'll look right through you.

Ich bin in Not. Wer will hilfen?

How Are You Spelling That?

The great director ____ ____ is in town and he is staying at the Royal Academy in Piccadilly. That's not the Royal Academy of Arts in Piccadilly, as Tim's agent explained to him. It's the Royal Academy Hotel in Piccadilly. Just a couple of blocks down from the Athenaeum, which in its turn is not that venerable hideout where bishops plot with masters of Cambridge colleges over the port and nuts while the pale winter sun slants through the dustmotes and lends a faint patina to the century-old leather worn almost threadbare by the arses of a thousand crafty old shirtlifters; it's just another very expensive and discreet hotel for rich Americans and Italians who like new places to sound like old places, and Tim Bone is not about to be intimidated by the Royal Academies and Athenaeums of this world, especially the fake ones.

Nor is he about to be intimidated by the ____ ____s of this world ... but here he hesitates, and takes a right up Half Moon Street. He's a little early, and a turn around the block will help to get his head straight. The thing is, there is only one ____ ____. People go to see ____ ____ pictures because they are ____ ____ pictures. Always did. ____ ____ never has to fight to get his name above the title. Because ____ ____ above the title is what sells the picture, to those who want to see that kind of picture. Not everybody wants to see that kind of picture, but enough of them do. ____ ____ has made one picture a year, sometimes two, for over thirty years now. He has never made the same picture twice, but you can come into one of his pictures anywhere, even channel-hopping drunk in a hotel room, and within thirty seconds you know you're watching a ____ ____.

Tim Bone is ____ ____'s kind of actor, he knows he is. He likes to be given room to run, and ____ ____ is a director who gives his actors room to run. With Tim Bone in the part, you get the characterisation, but you get a big piece of Tim Bone too. He's taken scenes away from leading actors just by sitting still and thinking into the camera. He is still only twenty-six – most people think he is twenty-two or three – and he is one of the hottest young actors in Europe just now. He has not been in a good picture yet, or a picture that has made any money, but there is a good buzz about him. He does not personally give a shit about this, of course. He just wants to do good work with fellow artists and craftsmen he respects. Such as ____ ____.

Tim's agent tried to sound very casual when he told Tim that ____ ____ wanted him to come in and talk, but Tim could hear his voice trembling. It's just going to be a casual chat, nothing specific, the great director has seen a little of Tim's work and liked it, and he likes to keep up with the new people, that's all. But Tim's agent knows, Tim knows, what everybody knows, that ____ ____ is looking for the leads for his next picture. His next picture is *Le Rouge et le Noir*. He has a great screenplay by Stephen St John Coke which he is going to hack to pieces himself before throwing it to his company as a basis for improvisation. The money is Italian, American and Japanese, and it is all there, everyone says so. Brando is doing to do one of his five-minute cameos. It's a very big deal.

That's OK with Tim. He'll wander in and say hello, and listen to what ____ ____ has to say, and let ____ ____ get a look at him. If the great director likes what he sees, and if Tim feels he can make a contribution in the role, well, fine. If not, that's fine too; there are plenty of other fellow artists and craftsmen keen to do good work with Tim Bone. He hasn't done any special preparation. His agent wasn't able to get hold of a copy of Coke's screenplay for love or money, so Tim has had to speed-read the whole fucking novel in the Penguin Classics edition, and fucking hard going it was too. He won't tell the great director he's read it, he doesn't want to sound too keen. He'll let the great director tell him about it, and ask him startlingly intelligent questions, showing an uncanny instinctive grasp of the surge and flow of the narrative, and a natural sympathy for the leading character with his curious mixture of calculation and impulsiveness. And ____ ____ will understand that Tim Bone can do the business.

Julien Sorel, he murmurs to himself as he strolls down Curzon Street. Julien Sorel . . . Julien Sorel . . . Julien Sorel. He walks past an expensive shop window full of handmade chocolates in decorated baskets, a *porte-cochère*. The streetlights blink and flicker as he turns into an alley, he feels the thin misty rain on his face . . . yes, that's how it should be; thin misty rain on his face as he steps out to meet his death. Julien Sorel. Tim Bone as Julien Sorel. 'Tim Bone *is* Julien Sorel, in ____ ____'s *Le Rouge et le Noir* . . . in his eyes we see reflected all the pure blue of the heavens, and all the filth of the road beneath our feet . . .'

The girl who hesitates towards him in the little square is about twenty years old and sweetly pretty under her umbrella. French, probably. Tim'll help out, Tim knows his way round. He smiles encouragingly at her, thinking immediately that he does this too often, he's too eager to help, to anxious to be liked, he has to keep his sense of difficulty, his sense of danger: Mickey Rourke didn't get where he is today by helping young ladies across the street, after all.

She comes up quite close to him and murmurs something that he doesn't quite catch.
    'Sorry, what?' he says.
    'I was wondering if you'd like to sleep with me,' she says, looking up shyly into his face.

And for a moment it feels so right, so true. Something about his hard, gaunt, vulnerable loneliness has drawn her to him . . . or perhaps she knows his work and has always thought that if she ever came face to face with him she would hesitate tremulously towards him and . . . but here she is, now, and what an extraordinary, charged moment it is. He

197

has been invited into bed by girls before, of course, some of them nearly as lovely as this one; but never before by a total stranger. Never by one whose very first words went straight to the heart of the matter. And her voice is sweet and low, her gaze steady and sincere, her smiling mouth telling as much of friendliness and humour as it does of passionate abandon ... and he has to be at ____ ____'s hotel in three minutes, for what might turn out to be the most momentous meeting of his professional life. What a poignant moment. *Mordant*. He is pierced. He is torn. The peaks of ambition, the yawning crevasse of love. What a, what a *European* moment. Worthy of, of ... yes, fuck it – Stendhal himself!

All that in one moment; and in the next, the desolate thump of commonsense.

'I'm sorry,' he says. 'Got an appointment, mustn't be late.' He is enraged with himself for being so embarrassed.

'Shame,' she says gently, and moves away towards a tall guy in a bowler hat who is sheltering in a shop doorway.

Shepherds Market. Of course. How could he be so clownishly, ludicrously ... ? It feels so right, so true *bollocks* ... something about his hard, gaunt, vulnerable *bollocks* ... extraordinary, charged *arseholes*!

Come on, think positive, he exhorts himself as he strides back down the hill towards Piccadilly. Any day now you might get offered something that needs a childlike sense of wonder and romance, or an intuitive understanding of what it's like to be an idiot, and you'll be right in there. And – and – yes, of course. If the vibes are good with____ ____, there is a way to tell that little anecdote that will go straight to the heart of the director *and* the picture. Somehow make it clear in a wry, Gallic, self-reflective way that it wasn't simply a choice between a fuck and a buck. It was a graceful acknowledgement that while there might be many women in a man's life, the world holds only one____ ____. Oh, brilliant, Tim. And will you be telling him that before licking between his toes, or after? Best to leave it out altogether. After all, nobody saw what just happened. Only you. Get in there.

Round the corner, up two steps, *bop* on the swing door, straight through without breaking stride and on up to the desk, using the hard springy walk he pioneered in *Gimme Some Skin*. The woman behind the desk looks Thai or something; long neck, high white blouse, something about her that suggests massage parlour or nose job clinic to Tim. She has her head down and she is writing something in a book and Tim stares at her hard to make her look up at him. She doesn't want to look up until he has spoken to her but he is going to make her look up and then speak to her. Out of the corner of his eye he is aware of a couple of guys looking at him. Hotel guys. Stuffed suits. Tim doesn't mind. They can look if they like. He is dressed conservatively with just a hint of flair: clean white T-shirt. 501s. Docs. And the six hundred quid cashmere coat with the ripped pocket hanging loose.

And now she does look up.

'How can I help you, sir?'
  'I've come to see＿＿ ＿＿. My name is Tim Bone.'
  She looks at him apprehensively.
  'Tin Bun?'
  'Tim Bone.'
  'Tim Bum.'
  'Tim *Bone*.'
  Christ, the sweat is pouring down his back, he can feel it.
  'Tin *Bone*?'
  'Near enough.'

She looks up at him. She looks ready to dissolve into angry tears.
  'I'm very sorry, sir, I am trying to get it just right.'
  'That's all right,' he hears himself saying. 'Don't worry. Just one of those names that's, you know, hard to hear. And I mumble.'
  Total bafflement.
  'You are humble?'
  'It doesn't *matter*.'
  Jesus Christ. How would Mickey Rourke handle this one? What does it matter how Mickey Rourke would handle this

one, he upbraids himself savagely. Mickey Rourke is just another dangerous young actor, just another fellow craftsman; we are all unique, and Tim Bone can handle this in his own inimitable way, i.e. by making a total prat of himself.

The young woman is looking frightened again and he forces himself to smile at her.

'And who are you coming to see, sir?'

'____ ____.'

'I'm sorry?'

'____ ____.'

She flips through some cards.

'And you think he is staying here?'

'I know he's staying here.'

She flips through the cards again.

'You are quite sure, sir?'

'*Yes.*' Christ. He hasn't walked into the Athenaeum by mistake, has he? 'This is the Royal Academy, isn't it?'

'Oh, yes, sir.'

'Have another look. Please.'

She flips through the cards again in a dejected sort of way.

'What did you say his name was, sir?'

'____ ____.'

'How are you spelling that, sir?'

He writes it down. She reads it, and smiles for the first time. She has a very sweet smile. She picks up the telephone and the actor can hear a woman's voice at the other end. The receptionist tells this woman that Mr Tim Bomb is here to see Mr ____ ____. The woman at the other end says something inaudible to Tim.

'Will you go up please?' says the Thai receptionist. 'The fourth floor. Room 404. The lift is there.'

They gaze at each other happily for a moment. Together they've cracked it. She too, in her way, is a fellow artist, and it's been great to work with her.

'Thank you for all your help,' he says, without irony.

'You're welcome,' she says. 'Have a nice evening.'

He has to share the lift with a thick-set Chinese man with what looks like a formidable erection, but Tim Bone can cope with that, no problem. He feels unaccountably good again, he feels like a man who has come through. The Chinese man gets out at three, and Tim proceeds alone to four, giving himself hardeye in the mirror, composing himself.

On four, the carpet is thick, the corridor hushed. Everything seems to be pale green, and the air feels oddly thick. He can feel a slight pressure against his ears and hear a faint high singing sound, as if he is walking underwater. The door of 404 wavers towards him. The numbers are golden. He can hear someone coughing inside. He knocks on the door.

The coughing stops. Nothing else happens. He waits for what seems like a long time then raises his hand to knock again and the door opens suddenly. He stares into the face of a woman in her forties with a lot of tear-stained make-up, wearing a fur coat over an embroidered black silk slip.

'Thank Christ,' she says. 'Are you the doctor? Where's your bag?'

'I'm not a doctor,' he says. 'I'm not sure whether I'm in . . . my name's Tim Bone. I've come to see ＿＿ ＿＿.'

She stares at him for a moment, then her face clears.

'Oh, right. Tim Burn. I know he wants to see you . . . we all loved you in, ah . . . look, come in, why don't you?'

Tim has done interviews in hotels before, but always in offices or in hotel suites that looked like offices. Room 404 is a bedroom, and looks like a bedroom. There is a very unmade bed, its rumpled pink sheets stained with what might be red wine. There is a large trolley piled high with what looks like the remains of several meals. There are some pizza cartons, and some bottles partly full of Scotch whisky, bourbon, vodka, tequila, Coke and other things. And there are three people. The woman who let him in; another woman, also in a fur coat but with what looks like a proper dress on underneath, sprawled in an easy chair with her eyes shut and her legs wide apart; and a small nondescript man with an untidy beard who is sleeping fitfully on the sofa. His face is very pale and gleaming with sweat. His eyelids are half open and Tim is able to see that his eyes are turned up. He does not look well at all. There is no sign of ____ ____ but he can hear someone coughing behind a closed door at the far end of the room.

'You want a drink, Tim?' says the woman who let him in. He accepts a beer. The coughing from the bathroom subsides.

'I think we all got, I dunno, food poisoning or something? I'm uh . . . Marie. And that there is Loretta. She killed a guy, can you believe that? Jimmy's not so good, I think he's awful sick, Tim, I'm worried about him.'

'He doesn't look well at all,' says Tim.

'What, *him*? That's not *Jimmy*. I thought you said you came to see Jimmy, I thought you said you *knew* Jimmy.'

'____ ____ is called Jimmy?'

'By his friends,' she says. 'Thought everybody in the whole world knew *that*.'

'So, er, who is that?'

'That? *Him*? That's just a writer, honey. He's called, uh . . . Ray? Ron? No. Rob Rust? Something like that. Jimmy was gonna have him do a polish, but I don't think he's gonna be able to give us what we want.'

She stares thoughtfully at the writer for a moment.

'A guy like that, he couldn't even polish ass with his tongue,' she says.

Tim thinks that there is something strange about that phrase, but he can't place what it is.

A huge racking spasm of coughing punctured by groans comes from behind the closed door, and the woman in the chair, the woman called Loretta, opens her eyes wide and stares at Tim.

'So who's this, the doctor?'

'No, honey, this is the actor.'

'Does he give back rubs?'

'I told you, honey, he's an *actor*.'

'Well let the actor speak. Do you give back rubs, actor?'

'I've, uh . . . it's been known,' says Tim modestly.

She stands up.

'OK, actor. Let's see what you can do.'

He is, he finds, only very mildly surprised to see her shrug off her coat and pull her dress over her head. She wears no underclothes. Her body is thin and strong-looking, and the draught made by her flying dress blows the smell of her like a gale into the actor's face. She smells very strong and at the same time very wholesome, like baking bread.

'Loretta,' says Marie wearily.

'Take no notice of her, actor,' says Loretta. 'Listen to me. This could be a very good deal for you. I am a big agent from the Coast. Do this right, and the world is your oyster.'

She walks three long strides across the room on her high heels, takes Tim's hand, and thrusts it between her legs. She feels warm, bristly, full of life. It doesn't seem to matter at all that she's a stranger; Tim knows instinctively that we are in a different world here, or in the same world at a different level, a level below the trivial and socially conditioned world of personality, a level where the life force flows unrestricted into any vessel adaptive enough to contain its energy, where it becomes impossible to say where Loretta ends and Tim begins, deep deep down, barely aware of the muffled echoes from the surface where Marie frets and _____ _____coughs behind his closed door, and the writer who couldn't even polish ass with his tongue sleeps his fitful sleep . . .

'Loretta, honey,' says Marie again. 'This is not a good idea. Leave the actor alone, honey. You'll have to forgive her, Tim. She's only been out of jail ten days.'

'It's all right, honestly,' says Tim. 'I don't mind.'

'See? He doesn't mind, Marie.'

'This is an English guy, honey. He's just being polite.'

'No, honestly, I'm not.'

'Listen, honey,' says Marie, to Tim this time. 'I am sure you are a very sweet guy, but you are forgetting what you are here for. I think that if poor Jimmy comes out of there and sees you like this he is not going to be happy with it at all.'

'Ah,' says Tim. 'You think so.'

'I know so,' says Marie, and as if to prove her right, another terrible echoing succession of coughs comes from behind the bathroom door.

'Loretta honey, you are putting this young man's career in jeopardy. You come down to the bar with me now, and we can have a nice quiet drink while Jimmy talks to the actor, and then Jimmy and the actor will come down to the bar and have a little drink with us, and you can have the actor later if you are still feeling horny, now is that a good plan?'

'Oh, I dunno. Yeah, I guess,' says Loretta in rather a whiney little-girl voice. 'So long, then, honey.'

She pulls her coat on, and the two women walk out of the room, Loretta with her dress still slung over her shoulder. It all happens so suddenly Tim feels lonely and bereft. He looks around the room. What a tip. Nowhere to sit. Nothing to read. God, that writer looks ill. And all very well, Jimmy talks to the actor, how is the actor going to get to talk to Jimmy if Jimmy is going to spend the entire night hawking in the bathroom? And what *is* all this *Jimmy* business anyway? Why can't he have his friends call him _____? Or even _____? Too much of this business seems to be devoted to making other people feel out of it. Mickey Rourke would probably have walked out hours ago.

The great director launches into another floor-shaking paroxysm, ending in a series of heartbreakingly pathetic groans. And . . . was that a sob? No. It's words. _____ _____ is calling to him in his famous harsh growling tones.

'Where the fuck is everyone?'

'Er . . . I'm here,' says Tim.

'Who the fuck are you?'

'I'm Tim Bone.'

Silence.

'You wanted to see me.'

More silence. Then the famous rumbling tones again, quieter this time.

'I'm awful sick. I think I'm dying.'

'I'm, er . . . sorry to hear that,' says Tim. Not too brilliant. 'Can I, er . . . can I do anything to help?'

A long pause.

'I don't know. Do you wanna try?'

'Yes, of course. I, I don't have any medical training . . .'

Another pause. The great director isn't coughing any more, but his breathing sounds terrible, even though the heavy door, hoarse and painful, with a chilling little gurgle at the end of each breath.

'Fuck . . . medical . . . training. Open the goddam door.'

Tim opens the door and gasps aloud.

The great director is lying on his back on the bathroom floor, dressed only in a pair of grey boxer shorts, and there is a hunting knife sticking out of his great hairy belly. He is trying to lift his head so that he can look directly into Tim's eyes.

'How . . . how did that happen?'

'Never mind that. I want you to pull it out.'

Tim starts to whimper, hears himself, tries to stop, can't, tries again, succeeds.

'I don't think, I don't think that's a good idea, I think, look, let me call an ambulance.'

'No time. No time. Do what I fucking tell you. Pull the fucker out.'

His famous blue eyes are blazing into Tim's. He is the great director. Tim is only an actor.

Slowly, trying to control the trembling, he reaches forward and closes his sweating fingers around the smooth warm leather handle. He's sure this is the wrong thing to do.

'Pull it out, Tim.'

He tries to lift it a little, slowly and gently, but feels a resistance, and a wave of faintness.

'Pull it *out*.'

He shuts his eyes and pulls hard, and the knife comes out, and so much blood, more blood than he would have thought possible, and the great director's body is jerking and trembling, and he doesn't know what to do to help him, to hold him together, to stop his poor life from flooding away across the sea of white tiles, and he presses his hands on to the wounds, but the blood leaps up between his fingers, and he

205

starts to sob, and he stands with the knife in his hand, soaked in the great director's blood, and now there are other men in the bathroom with them, and he has seen them somewhere before, yes, they are the hotel men, the stuffed suits from the foyer, and he turns to them, his arms spread wide, and both of them flatten themselves against the wall, and he understands, and drops the knife.

And later some more men come, and they ask him his name, and he tells them, and they ask him how he is spelling that.

Coming
Mince

She had been corresponding with him for months, and now that they were about to meet she was not sure whether she would be able to bear the excitement. She was not well. She had been in bed for three days with flu, had several times lifted the phone to cancel their appointment, but had not in the end been able to wait for his voice and hear his disappointment or anger or indifference. But today she was better. Wobbly, but intact. The strange, floating sensations, the muddy half-caught echoes of her waking dreams had receded back into the shadows. After a number of furious snorts of Otrivine her head felt unnaturally clear.

She was sitting in the tiny overheated foyer of the little cinema, watching the lift doors. It was a strange place to meet anyone, and not really like her idea of a cinema at all. It was on the fifth floor of a new block of shops and apartments, and the foyer was really just an apartment block landing, with a tiny ticket office opposite the lift, and a tiny bar next to the ticket office. The tiny bar and the tiny ticket office were staffed by Japanese; and the whole thing so much embodied her idea of what Japan must be like that for a moment or two she wondered whether she might be hallucinating again.

Every time the lift doors opened her heart jumped. Every time it was a man between the ages of twenty and seventy she found herself half rising from the seat, anxiously smiling, to greet him. She had seen photographs, of course, loads of them, but photographs can be so deceptive, and writers in particular, she had noticed, tend to choose photographs of themselves which look not only younger, slimmer and nicer, but also cleverer, deeper, more thoughtful and more in control of the world than they appear in real life and three dimensions.

But, of course, when the lift doors opened for the tenth time, and it was him, she knew immediately, and knew how stupid she had been, because he looked exactly like himself, and not in the least like anybody else she had ever seen. She went to him and said, 'Hello, I'm Catherine.' She had to do this because she had not sent him a photograph of herself, and she was not famous, as he was. She had described herself: twenty-seven, five feet eight, long dark straight hair, black coat, blue jeans . . . there was not much more she could say to prepare him, without seeming grossly immodest.

'Oh,' he said. '*Are* you?' He seemed quite overwhelmed, as if there were somehow much more of her than he had bargained for.

They had both arrived early, and there was some time before the film began. They sat at the tiny bar and had a drink. He told her about his journey down from Derbyshire, which had been a succession of anxieties and frustrations and near-disasters. He only came to London twice a year, he said, at most, for meetings with his agent and his publishers. There had been nothing else to make it worth his while, he said. The words 'until now' hovered unspoken in the air between them.

He sipped whisky and talked about his life. It was all she had hoped for. There were no false notes: his world and the world of his stories were the same world, harsh, wry, compassionate, uncomfortable; a world, she suddenly found herself thinking, in which nobody giggled. And she felt a little stab of shame, because she really giggled quite a lot, off and on. And he even *looked* like his stories. His skin was stretched tightly over his bones, and despite its constant exposure to the weather – he actually wrote outdoors for nine months of the year – it had a raw, tender look about it, as if his world had been too harsh for it. His eyes, too, looked tired and red and sore, as if they had been held open and on the watch for too long, though their gaze when he looked at her directly was piercing, the irises a light – almost transparent – grey, the pupils tiny. And the photographs had caught very little of the quality of his short-cropped hair and beard, gingery fading into silver, like a fox in winter, glittering, wiry, electric, as if he could apprehend the world through each hair and whisker.

He never mentioned his wife and family. He spoke as if he lived quite alone.

Only one thing disappointed her: his response to her. He did not seem to give his full attention to what she said, though she felt it to be quite interesting and perceptive; she had, for example, seen exactly how he had combined elements of two of his neighbours into the figure of the Pigman in *Battery*, and used the same elements in a completely different way in *Divining*. But he nodded, almost impatiently, and then said, 'D'you know, your eyes really are violet, aren't they? There's no other word for that colour. I'd always imagined it to be a romantic fiction, never observed it in real life. I really think you have the most extraordinary eyes I've ever seen. I hope you don't mind my saying that.'

Well, no, of course she didn't exactly mind him saying that, but surely he must realise that it had been said to her before, several dozen times, in fact, and some of those times by people who had turned out to be complete bollockheads; it wasn't exactly the kind of observation you need a great writer for, was it? And she would have liked him to praise her for something she felt rather more responsible for. But against that, there he was in all his sensitivity, with his rawness and his fine-drawn intensity and his electric whiskers and everything; and it was good to know that he found her attractive. She was not quite sure yet exactly how she felt about him in that way. She thought she would like to touch him gently with her fingers. She had soft fingers. She thought that she might like to stroke the taut stretched skin over his bony forehead, and take his tense bony face between the palms of her hands; perhaps stroke his eyelids shut over his tired, sore

211

eyes. Perhaps lick his eyelids gently. Perhaps even give his eyes a little lick.

It was time to go into the film. She was wishing now that she had not agreed to his suggestion that they should see a film together on their first date – if date was what it was. They should have met in a restaurant, spent more time facing each other, more time looking, more time talking, more time listening. Now they were going to go into the dark and sit side by side watching a film. When she was thirteen she had gone to the cinema in Aldershot every Saturday afternoon with Alan Pugh. Alan Pugh had been her boyfriend and she loved him very much, and they always sat in the back row and snogged until her knickers were soaking wet. Going to the cinema as an adult had always carried with it a sense of lowered expectations.

Perhaps he might want to hold hands, but she doubted it. He didn't look like a hand-holding man. Anyway, in a funny sort of way, hand-holding, in the sense of sitting or walking side by side holding hands as distinct from taking someone's hand across the table in a restaurant, say, really came after shagging not before, once you were over fifteen. She thought she would give him a chance, though, and when Louis Malle's name came up she leaned over and whispered to the writer how much she loved Malle's films, thinking immediately what a wet, gushy, eager-to-please sort of thing to say that was; but it gave him a chance to take her hand, if he felt so inclined; it gave him a chance to lean into her. But he didn't. He stayed still and rigid. And more than that. He seemed more than tense – extra bony, as if his ribs were on the outside of his skin instead of on the inside. Or one of his ribs, at least. But that was ridiculous. What could it be? Surely the writer wasn't wearing a corset?

What with thoughts like these going through her mind, and the tense, hunched figure of the writer by her side, it took a little while before she could surrender herself to the film. But after a while she did, couldn't help herself, melted through the frame into the eyes of the poor baffled boys with their botched haircuts and their bony knees and their precarious happiness; and at the end the tears were streaming down her face . . . She supposed it might partly be down to the weakening effect of the flu.

The writer must have noticed her distress, but he made no comment, perhaps out of tact.

They went to a cheap Indonesian restaurant. It was very crowded, and a sweating harassed-looking waiter led them through tables of fat noisy people bulging out of their territory with their big coats and bags and noisy laughter. It was strange: half the people in the restaurant seemed to be Germans and Swedes in transit, with rucksacks and cases and huge sausagey holdalls.

She wondered briefly what the writer had done with his luggage, whether he had reserved a hotel room, what the end of the evening would be, and then let it all slide. Suddenly she felt too weak to cope. The waiter led them across a ridiculous, arched, cardboardy bridge over a fake stream to a tiny table.

As soon as they sat down she realised that the restaurant was very hot as well as very crowded, and that she did not feel hungry at all. The writer professed total ignorance of Indonesian cuisine while the waiter chafed politely at their side. Finally she ordered some things, pointing at the menu here and there in a vague smiley sort of way, not quite sure what she was doing. Someone seemed to be turning the volume up and down, and the temperature control. The writer appeared to have totally abdicated responsibility. She began to think that she might have to ask the writer if he could just put her in a cab and forget the whole thing, but then the waiter came back with a couple of large whiskies she couldn't remember ordering. She drank one of them off, and felt better immediately.

'Drink up!' she said to the writer, and he did what he was told. It seemed to have a galvanising effect on him; to go straight to his brains and whiskers. He leaned across the table,

213

stared deeply into her eyes and began to interrogate her about her life. No worries now about whether she had his full attention or not. It was her childhood that interested him most, and no detail was too small or trivial for him. His piercing eyes permitted no escape. He made her remember things she had not thought about for years: names she thought she had forgotten, feelings she had thought she would never feel again. She began to realise that one of the reasons why she had responded so passionately to the writer's stories was that she too had known the poverty and the anger and the endless pointless *wanting* that he wrote about. But he didn't want her abstract nouns, he didn't want her analysis, he didn't want her philosophy, he wanted her life, in detail, minute by minute. He wanted to hear how she had tried to wear her dead auntie's ginger suit and carry it off with style because it was either that or her brother's parka – no money to buy her anything of her own ever; he wanted how she had stolen Alison Price's fountain pen and stabbed her with it when she had been found out; he wanted her and Robert Atkins, sitting under a shared anorak in the corner of the infants' playground in the rain. He wanted her life so much it almost felt like love.

And she let him have it. She told him anything he wanted to know. She let him right in there.

And when it was the end of the evening she went back with him to his hotel. He could have afforded somewhere good, but he had chosen one of the big cheap hotels near the railway terminus, that catered for cut-price tours.

When they got out of the taxi she was made privy to the mystery of the external rib, or writer's corset. He had been carrying his room key with him, and the key, large in itself, was attached to an even larger metal contraption, about a foot long and rather like a meat skewer with a metal plate at the end . . . somehow she associated it with war injuries; her grandfather had been supposed to have a metal plate in his skull. She wondered why the writer had carried it round with him all the evening but she did not ask him. Some sort of convention about who asked the questions and who gave the answers seemed to have been firmly established.

Her nervousness came back as they went up in the lift. The only other passenger was a thickset Chinese man with what looked like a formidable erection. Nobody spoke.

The corridor was long and the writer's room was right at the end of it. He wrestled in silence for a moment with his extra rib, and then the door opened.

She was very nervous by now and she hardly glanced at the room. It seemed to be mostly brown and beige. Head down, she went into the bathroom and locked the door. She found that she was feeling rather strange again. She took some of her clothes off and sat on the toilet seat, too tense to piss. Then she remembered how he had been too shy to order in the restaurant, and so in awe of the Irish hotel staff that he had been too nervous to check his key in and out. She felt tender towards him again, and her bladder relaxed. Then she splashed a lot of water on her face, brushed her teeth with the toothbrush she had brought out with her just in case, and opened the door.

The bedroom looked different. The light was murkier, and surely the room itself had got much larger, or had she not noticed how large it was when they first came in? The light was so dim that it was difficult to make out exactly how long the room was, but there were at least a dozen beds in it, stretching away in a long row, and many of them (she noticed with only mild surprise) were occupied. Some of the beds had one person in them and some of them had couples in them. Some of the couples appeared to be making love, but quietly and slowly, as if underwater. One or two people were looking towards her and the writer, propped up on elbows or peering over magazines, but nobody seemed to be avidly interested. She and the writer did not appear to be the main attraction. Live and let live seemed to be the order of the night in this hotel.

The writer was sitting on the edge of the bed in his pants getting something out of a suitcase. His body was just as she had imagined it: thin, narrow-shouldered, tense, almost boyish. Bluey-white stretched skin. Nipples and areolae that might have been smudged on with a child's crayon they were so flat and pale.

She took the rest of her clothes off, making no attempt to hide herself from him or from the other shadowy occupants of the strange dormitory. Her body was the least of her anxieties. Her breasts were high, her waist and legs were slender, her round bottom was as firm as a boy's. She got into the bed and lay waiting for him.

He seemed to be putting something on, something that fastened around his waist. The doorkey with its strange attachments appeared to be part of it. It was made of stainless steel, and it looked like some sort of scientific instrument. She was frightened. He looked up at her and touched her hand.

'It's all right,' he said. 'Haven't you ever seen one of these before? It's a sextant.'

Surely that was wrong? A sextant was something different, wasn't it? It wasn't anything to do with sex, it was to do with . . . navigation, or something like that. *Treasure Island. Mutiny on the Bounty*.

'You see, I have to examine you first,' he said. 'I'm sure you understand that, don't you? I promise it won't hurt.'

He seemed very sure of what he was talking about, and there was nothing in his manner that suggested he might be lying, might want to hurt her more than anything else. She lay back and smiled at him rather nervously, and he squeezed her hand. Then he climbed on to the bed and knelt over her carefully, one knee on each side of her body, and it began.

The idea seemed to be to pass the instrument slowly over every inch of her body from every angle, rather as his ques-

216

tions in the restaurant had explored every year of her life. And it did not hurt, exactly. The metal was cold against her skin and sometimes the pressure gave her a little discomfort, but while it could not possibly be described as pleasurable, it was easily tolerable. He praised her constantly, telling her how sensible and patient she was being, and that she would soon see how worthwhile the process was; and gradually she found herself relaxing. And she was not surprised at all when he moved to an internal examination. Again, it was not exactly pleasant. She had to help him insert the instrument; but he was, so far as she could tell, as gentle and considerate as he could be in its application.

But it was not what she had expected, and it was not what she had wanted. She had wanted to do something for him; she had wanted them to be able to do something together. She reached up and touched his face, she stroked his cheek, his poor sore-looking eyelids. She stroked and kneaded his wiry chest and his flat belly. She could see his penis, thin, blue-veined, tense and raw-looking, straining upwards in its stainless steel cage, and she reached her fingers towards it, but he pushed her hand away and groaned as if he were in pain.

'What's the matter?' she said.

He was staring at her as if he was in terror, trembling all over. Then his eyes watered and he began to gasp, his body arching and jerking over her. He was trying to speak but he did not seem to be able to get the words out. She looked down the room and called out, but no one was paying attention.

Then the stuff began to spurt out of the end of his penis. Thick stuff, viscous knobbly stuff, pink and grey and lumpy and greasy. At first she thought she had never seen anything like this stuff in her life, but then she realised that she had, she had seen it coming out of machines in butchers' shops; she had eaten more of it than she cared to remember as a child, both at home and in school dinners. It was mince, it was mince, it was half-cooked, fatty minced meat. The writer was coming mince, gasping and jerking, unable to stop the

217

great gobbets of mince from flying out of the end of his penis all over the bed, all over her, all over himself, all over everything. She had to help, the writer was in desperate trouble, she had to help, but she didn't know what to do. Together they tried to catch the mince and collect it in the cage of the sextant, but it was a hopeless task; it kept slipping through the stainless steel bars, and in any case, there was too much of it – it just kept coming, more and more of it, and she began to be afraid that it would not stop until she was buried in it, until the whole room was full of the writer's mince, until there was nothing left of the writer and nothing left of her but the mince that was still coming out with no sign of abating.

More Or Less
Anything at
More Or Less
Any Time

From: the C.L.B.
To: all staff.

Christine darling:

This is all we seem to know at the moment. It is not much, but maybe it is something.

Most viruses that people are aware of work by planting a Trojan Horse in COM and EXE files. These Trojan Horses extend the length of the file and are frequently known by the number of extra bytes they add.

When any COM or EXE file which is infected is run on a PC it can in principle take some or all of the following actions, always or sometimes:

– scan the entire hard-disc for COM and EXE files and add the Trojan Horse to each one if it is not already present.

– leave code resident in the PC which will modify any COM and EXE files on any floppy disc that is read or written onto that PC, or on any remote file-server that is later accessed.

– identify programmes explicitly designed to detect and remove data viruses, and infect them with new varieties of Trojan Horses.

– activate a TIME-BOMB capable of doing MORE OR LESS ANYTHING AT MORE OR LESS ANY TIME.

Some Possibilities for Discussion.

We have already exploited analogies in which the invasion of data storage and retrieval systems has been compared to diseases of the viral kind invading the human immune system.

We have raised in a tentative way an exploratory approach to psychological and emotional dysfunction amongst sophisticated metropolitan bollockheads, interpreting their plight as being analogous to (say) a WP program which has been colonised by The Moose.

Christine, Christine, increasingly I have been prey to dreadful notions. Not that you and I are the unwitting hosts to some new and fatally encompassing data virus parasite growths . . .

No . . . that *we* may be living in and on some poor bastard's brain without being aware of it at all!

I mean, how can you tell, Christine? How can you bloody well tell?

We may be living inside a time-bomb which has been activated to do more or less anything at more or less any time.

Things that we can do about it

Christine Christine, they gave me this job because I was a clever-looking bloke, but I think that all we can do now is to listen and look and smell and see if we like the taste of things.

If we drag ourselves very slowly and carefully towards the doorway, I think we shall find that the sky is becoming a little lighter and that the air is a little fresher and that there is even a breeze blowing towards us over the rank marshes . . .

and if we keep telling each other stories at least we'll have some evidence we might still be alive.

The idea was to drive non-stop all the way from Wroclaw to Battersea. It was my idea and it was a stupid one. I told her that it was all about deadlines and meetings in London, but really it was about her; it was about her and me; I didn't want to be in Wroclaw with her any longer, left out on the fringes of every conversation, dependent on the scraps of translation she tossed me from that language I had been too lazy to learn. Nor did I want us to stop in Germany, either of the Germanies, she had family and friends in East and West; Wittenberg, Bremen, Dresden, Bochum. Wittenberg, Bremen, Dresden, Bochum. The first time she told me the names of those towns I thought they sounded beautiful together, like a peal of bells or a litany. Now they were just four places to avoid. Four places where I might lose her.

We took it in strict turns; we were always meticulously fair with each other. Four hours on, four hours off. And there was time out too, when we stopped to eat, relieve ourselves, wash, even shower, in one or two lucky places. Time out, but not time out from each other. The only time she was out of my sight was when she was in the *Damen*. I felt that I would fall apart if I could not reach out my hand and touch her. I suppose she must have felt like a prisoner.

She escaped into sleep when I had my stints at the wheel. I didn't. Couldn't. And that was not about her and me, that was just about me. I have always been a terrible passenger. Not a back-seat driver – I don't nag or say things – I just seem to have to watch the road; it's as if I'm thinking that if I take my eyes off the road ahead for a second, the car will crash. I have never had that gift of being able to trust myself entirely to another person.

So I must have been very tired already when we crossed the border near Eisenach. Bautzen, Meissen, Leipzig, already nothing but the names themselves, white on green, looming up and fading away, floating behind us in the long night. They had opened up the borders two months ago. No more of those tedious searches, checking every paperback against a list as long as a mail order catalogue. The guard had taken the briefest glance at my passport, glanced in at her as she lay sleeping on the back seat, laughed, and waved me on. But I looked behind me too, to the shape on the back seat under the rug, perhaps to see what he was laughing at. There was nothing, in a sense, to see, just a dark shape, the sort of shape a sleeping woman makes, head down in the dark corner, knees drawn up, the bold, high curve of the hip an authenticating signature.

But it didn't look right.

And yet I drove on.

People are always telling you why they do things. I find their confidence misplaced. If you want to know the truth, I find their breezy certainties disgusting. I am very often unable to explain to myself or anyone else why I do the things that I do.

I am quite willing to go through the motions: I was very tired and very short of sleep. I might have been hallucinating. I might have *thought* I was hallucinating when I perceived the shape on the back seat as somehow the wrong shape. I might have been too tired to care. I might have been too scared to look.

I don't know why I drove on, but I did drive on, and I went on driving.

When I was too tired to drive any further, I pulled off the road and I slept for an hour at the wheel.

I never looked behind me again. Once or twice I spoke to her, telling her that it was all right if she wanted to go on sleeping; I was happy to drive all the way, it had been my idea, after all, ha ha. She did not reply when I spoke to her; of course I know why, now, but then she might simply have been asleep. And in any case, how could it possibly have happened? How could I possibly have imagined what was on the back seat? How could it have been done?

I drove on to the ferry at Ostend and I left her still sleeping on the back seat down below on the car-deck, and walked up on top. No one was out there except me. It was pouring with rain and the wind was high. I remember thinking that it would be easy just to let go and allow the wind to take me over the rail. Then I went down to the bar. I drank my drinks and made my mind blank, and after a while I slept, despite the storm. I woke refreshed as the ferry docked, and drove up the motorways through the night, making Battersea by four am.

I drove into the garage and the door closed behind me. I switched off the engine. It sounded very quiet in the garage when I had done that. I sat in the front seat for a while, thinking that in a moment I would turn round and take the rug off and see what it was, see what was the matter with her. But after five minutes or so I found myself getting out of the car, locking it, and going upstairs to my flat. I had a wash and went straight to bed.

I woke at about ten and went in to work. My newspaper has its offices on the south side of Chelsea Bridge, just five minutes' walk from my flat. I never drive to work.

By three in the afternoon I had had enough of that. I had shifted a lot of paper in the morning, but since lunchtime my thoughts had been returning to the garage. I walked home, unlocked the garage and went inside, closing the door behind me, and took my first proper look at the shape on the back seat.

It was as I had thought – something was wrong. She didn't

look right. I remember feeling very cold as I reached for a corner of the rug, took hold of it, and pulled it off her.

It was not her at all. It was a doll. It was a life-sized doll, made out of some soft mundane material: sacking, I suppose you would have to call it, except that the weave was closer and finer than the weave of most sacks that I have seen. It felt soft and warm under my fingers. It was stuffed to the consistency of a home-made rag doll, and it looked as if it had been made with some skill and ingenuity; some, but not all that much. Its most impressive feature as a representation of the female form was the strong, noble curve of the hip. Little attempt had been made to represent the subtle curves of arms and legs, the heartstoppingly delicate engineering of the human wrist, say. The limbs, to be frank, were like saus-ages. The hair was black and straight and long, like her hair. The eyes were represented as being closed, or perhaps demurely lowered, by two shallow arcs of long black eye-lashes. If it had been on a smaller scale – a few inches long, say, instead of a few feet long – it would have made a charm-ing present for a little girl, or even a big girl. As it was, though, taking up the back seat of my car with its knees drawn up to its lifeless chest, taking the space and taking the place of my vanished lover, it was a worrying, even a frightening presence. Less than human, but distressingly, unfathomably less, like a corpse. It took me quite an effort of will to grasp it and lift it out of the car and carry it upstairs to the flat.

It was not until I had laid it out on the living room floor that I noticed its most striking feature. Most dolls, I suppose, are quite smooth in the genital area: no attempt is made to represent the primary sexual organs, even in those Barbies and Cindies and so on, who are imagined as adolescent, and sport smooth little hillocks on their pink plastic chests. No one had attempted to mould breasts for this doll. Not even a pair of coin-sized darns to represent nipples. But it wore a fine bush of black glistening pubic hair, coarser than the hair on its head and curlier, and between its parted legs I saw that someone had . . . I noticed to my astonishment . . . I was not a little taken aback to . . .

Somebody had made a cunt for it. Sorry. I find this just as painful as you do, probably very much more so. And I'm afraid I have to go into more detail than this. It wasn't a formal gesture, a reference, a sign, an indicator, a stand-in, a metaphor for a cunt. To all intents and purposes it was the thing itself. At least, its outward visible parts, its external labia to be precise, looked like it. It was quite different in scope, ambitions, intentions and execution from the rest of the doll. It was breathtakingly lifelike. If it wasn't a real cunt, it looked like a first-class working model of one. And not just any old cunt, either. It was *her* cunt, her dear cunt. It was hers.

I don't like writing down what I did next, and I didn't like doing it very much, but I had to know. I shut my eyes, and I stroked it gently and patiently with the tips of my fingers, as I had done so many times before, and slowly and gradually began to ease the lips apart, and felt her begin to open like a flower under my fingers. I stopped then, but I knew that if I continued it would open fully to me, and I knew it would soften and moisten and cling and draw me inside.

I stood up. I didn't know what to do with the doll. It felt wrong for it to be lying there naked on the rug in the draught coming from under the door. I lifted it up and stood face to face with it for a moment. It was the same height as me. The same height as her. Five feet seven. Short for a man, rather tall for a woman. She used to stand face to face with me and rub noses and laugh. The doll had no nose.

I tried sitting her in an armchair, but I felt uncomfortable with that. No matter how I arranged the limbs, she looked as if she was waiting for something to be done to her. And there was another thing: I didn't know whether she was she or it.

The next thing I did was very strange indeed, but it felt

perfectly normal at the time. I went to the chest and got out one of my American shirts, and cut off the loop from the middle of the back. She had often laughed at my fondness for these shirts, which incidentally had nothing to do with the hanging loop, though she thought it had, or pretended she did. European shirts have the loop on the inside of the collar. My American shirts had the loop in the middle of the back, between the shoulder blades. She used to say that I could hang myself up on the back of the door when I felt too drunk to put myself to bed. When I had cut the loop off the shirt I got a needle and thread and sewed it to the doll, in the same place, in the middle of the back, between where her shoulder blades would have been if she had had any.

Then I hung her on the back of the door.

I was trying to avoid thinking about what this doll meant, which was glaringly obvious. The doll was a message from her to me. She had substituted this doll for herself, because that was all I needed of her. She was telling me that the only thing about her that was real for me was her cunt.

I sat in the armchair and I stared at the doll for a long time, and after a while I started to weep. I think I was weeping not only for the loss of her, but for the unfairness of it all: I felt that I had been brutally and wilfully misunderstood. It had not been like that for me at all. It had been her that I loved. I felt just as much anger as sorrow.

Over the next few days I did some sensible things as well as some deranged things. There were two or three dozen numbers I could ring, all over Europe, the telephone numbers of our friends, of her friends, of her relatives. None of them said that they had seen her, or heard from her. Of course I had no way of telling whether they were speaking the truth or not. If they asked me why I was ringing, I said that she had left me, and that I wanted to get in touch with her – I wanted her back. I didn't say that I was worried about her, that I was worried that she had met with some injury, or even death. In fact I was not worried about her in that way at all. I had a very strong feeling that she was in the world and that she was alive and well and happy to be away from me, and quite content to leave her cunt with me. And her friends and relatives did not seem to be worried in that way either. So perhaps they did know where she was. As I say, I had no way of knowing.

I went round to her flat several times – she had always insisted on keeping her own place, and sometimes liked to spend the night alone there – but it was clearly empty. After a while an estate agent's board went up outside. I phoned the agents, who said that they had been instructed by a solicitor. I went to see the solicitor but she said that she was not able to give me any information about her client.

The quality of my work was affected, but so far as I was able to tell nobody was much aware of it except myself. I took to leaving the office early and going back to the flat. Sometimes I would work, and sometimes I would sit and look at the doll.

Eventually, of course, I fucked it. It was terrible. It felt exactly like being inside her cunt again, as I had known it would, but the rest of it felt absurd and mad and frightening. I shut my eyes tight and tried to will her into being, tried to see her face, but she didn't come.

After that, I wanted to destroy the doll.

But I couldn't do that.

My head ached all the time. I thought that it might feel better if I threw the doll out. Sneaked out at night and threw it into a skip. I imagined myself doing it, but each time I imagined it, I couldn't walk away from the skip and leave her behind. So she stayed where she was. If I couldn't destroy her or throw her out, somehow I was going to have to let her go by herself.

* * *

I was so anxious about bringing you back to the flat, that first time. I thought you would take one look at her and walk out of my life forever. But you didn't seem to notice her at all. You just looked at me.

I told you that first time that I was looking for someone to love, and you took both my hands, and put the tips of my fingers inside the top of your blouse so that I could feel your breasts. I was absolutely astonished and at the same time felt that I had known exactly what was going to happen.

When I turned and looked at the door the doll had gone.

The New
Baboon

The trouble was, that if I kept the females all together in one place they quarrelled with each other and got on my nerves – or, worse than that, ganged up on me and refused to groom me properly, and sat around criticising my jumping and swinging style and the size of the coconuts I brought home.

But if I kept them all in separate trees and caves it was difficult to see what they were getting up to. Some of my older sons, Ong and Grd in particular, were becoming increasingly ambitious to perform *upoopoo* with my females, and some of the younger females seemed to me to be encouraging Ong and Grd in these efforts to subvert my domination. It became necessary for me to rise very early in the morning, and be the last baboon to retire for sleep at night. And it was increasingly wearisome for me to have to call and display and make *grawgraw* at the young males every single day, and even, on occasion, give heavy *bangbang* to one or another of them.

They were too stupid, or too contentious one against the other, to join forces against me: if I was forced to give *bangbang* to Ong, for example, Grd would watch in a state of excitement and delight, leaping up and down and chittering and pulling on his dogo. But if they were too stupid for that, they were too stupid also to see that their *awa* was to leave the pack, and wander alone until they could find their own females and become senior baboons in their turn.

It was my duty, my *awa* too, to keep my sons from my females. This was so that my offspring would be big and strong like me. And – yes, you are no doubt there before me – grow up into uppity bonkers like Ong and Grd and make their father's life a misery in their turn.

The life of a baboon is full of cruel ironies.

Besides my females and my uppity sons, I also had to worry about the loneboys; fully-grown males who had left their pack or been driven from it in their first maturity, and now travelled the coastline where the jungle reaches down to the silver beach, looking for a pack to conquer and make their own.

I had once been a loneboy, and had won my females from a terrible old bangerboy called Walt in a fight that had frightened all the baboons within ten daynights' walking of the Blue Rock hollow. And since then I had made twenty-seven successful defences of my territory against wandering loneboys. Sometimes it had been enough merely to display and make *grawgraw* and show them my dogo. More often it was necessary to give them heavy *bangbang*. Sometimes tear them with my main teeth, even. Only once did I have to kill a loneboy, and he was a crazy ape, crazy from drinking bad juice. We are not like the human men. A beaten baboon knows when he is beaten and he will ask to go away, and a strong baboon will let him go. Maybe the human men drink bad juice.

That was my life, a hard life, and full of little irritations and big worries too. And then one day the new baboon came along the shore from the West, and that was when my troubles really started.

I woke to hear my females chattering, and for once they had gathered closely round me, each one wanting to touch and snog and groom me. I looked around, and then I saw what they were chattering about. Only fifty jumps away, down by the sea, a new baboon, a big hungry loneboy, sitting on his gopa and displaying his dogo to my females. I felt a great weariness and irritation at having to prepare for another defence. No fear. This new baboon was big and hungry, yes, but nothing to me. One good *bangbang* on his head and he would understand that.

I shook my females off and stood up in all my bigness. He

did not move. I blew my face up and gave him *stiffhair* and *hardeye*. He showed me his main teeth. I kept my *hardeye* on him and I walked right down onto the beach, towards him, no back and forth, no shouting, no *grawgraw*; I was very meanbusiness and believe me I was doing bigboy walking. I wanted to get this thing over fast and get some peace and quiet. When I am two jumps from him I stop so that he can see all my meat. And I show him my main teeth and I let him hear my big noise and smell my fierce, fighty smell. All right then, loneboy. I come at him like a big wave – and he's not there! I am going *bangbang* on bare sand!

I heard my females chattering and I turned around. The lone-boy was running and wriggling among my females and they were going *chattersqueak looklook*, and then I saw he had captured one – he had captured Lpipi, a young, justready one . . . and I made big noise and went fast like a wind to catch him, but he was much too fast to catch, and he was carrying and pulling Lpipi up a high tree; and though she was going *chattersqueak* she was not fighting him, but holding round his back and helping him to climb; and I gave a big, fighty growl and I went up that tree after him, I was ready to fight him out of that tree and throw him on his head and break him, but he was such a climber that he was a long way ahead of me, and reached the top of the tree when I was only halfway up. And to my terrible shame and anger, when I looked at him, he was doing *upoopoo* with her, onetwothree, so fast that he had finished when I was still five jumps away, and he left her for me, and jumped himself to another tree, and so down to the beach, and away.

And so the days of my misery started. Every day, and some-times in the night, the new baboon would come; and every time he ran away when I went to fight him; and every time he was too fast for me to catch him; and every time he managed to steal Lpipi or one of the other young females; and every time he would perform *upoopoo* with one of them, sometimes two of them. After a time, I saw that there was little that I could do, for he would not behave like a true baboon and understand that he was not strong enough to take

237

my females from me. I stopped trying to chase him, and instead I kept my females with me all the time, so that he could not get at them. He would come to the beach, as he had done the first day, and sit on his gopa displaying his dogo, and all the females would go *chatterchatter looklook*, but I would not move, and he waited for Lpipi and the other just-readies in vain.

But in time I came to see that that was a failure too: kept all day and night together in a big huddle, the females quarrelled with each other and got on my nerves, or ganged up on me and refused to groom me properly, and talked about me without respect. I was unable to venture far to gather food, because of the loneboy. I never knew how far or how near he was hiding. Sometimes I only had to move ten jumps from my females, and I would turn to find him doing *upoopoo* with Lpipi or another one.

Worse still. Sometimes Lpipi and two or three of the other justreadies would steal away when I was dozing, would steal away on purpose to be with the loneboy, the new baboon, and do *upoopoo* with him, because they liked the way he did *upoopoo*. And after that a strange thing happened. I found that I did not want to do *upoopoo* as often as I had been used to doing it. When the new baboon had first come, I had wanted to do *upoopoo* more often than usual, perform it with every female every day, sometimes as much as ten times a day with some of them. But when he had been coming for many days I was weary with the worry of it all and I felt a sadness even in my dogo, and my head had a pain in it every day, even though no one had given it *bangbang*, and I could smell a sad smell, and I knew that it was mine. And after that, I could not do *upoopoo* at all.

One day I awoke and I felt different. The pain in my head had gone. My dogo was still hiding his head and I was still not able to do *upoopoo* but I did not care any more. And I did not want to take care of anyone except myself any more. I wanted to be alone. I was not ashamed of this. I understood it was my *awa* to leave the pack and go away by myself.

And that was what I did.

I travelled east, many daynights' walking. I kept to the shore-line, only going into the jungle to get food. It was hard to get food, because there were other packs, and they drove me away from the food, as I had driven other wandering, lonely baboons away from my food. I could have fought for the food, but I did not want to fight any more, I was tired of it. These packs were strange packs, I could not tell who was the leader; it seemed to me that the days of the senior baboon were over. I began to be sad again. I could not change from what I was. I did not want to become a baboon who won his food and his females by tricks and fast climbing, and I was tired of fighting. I did not want *upoopoo* any more. I took the nearest food from the lowest branches and I ate it without happiness. Sometimes I drank bad juice. And I smelt the sad smell again, and I knew that it was my smell.

One day I wanted to walk into the sea. This was a strange want. Baboons live near the sea but they do not go in it. We are not good swimmers and we don't eat fish. But I wanted to go in. I thought it might wash away my sad smell. And I walked into the sea a short way, until the water was as high as my dogo, and it seemed to me that my sad smell was not so strong. So I walked in further, but then a big wave came and I fell into the wet darkness and it felt like a huge leg had been thrust down my throat and I wanted to sleep in the middle of the pain, but then I wanted to fight the water until I could ask it to let me go, and it fought me and gave me heavy *bangbang*, and in the end tumbled me back on to the beach, nearly broken.

And it was there, on that beach, half drowned, choking, exhausted, near to death, that I met my future wife. My dear one. Her name is Leonora, and she will tell you herself how it came about.

*

My heart is too full for many words. Yes, I am engaged to be married. I am the happiest woman in the world, and I pity those who mock at me and shun me: I think they will never know the happiness I know.

One Sunday morning – it was the third of January last – I went with Mrs Pittenden to take the waters and indulge in a sea bath in the warm currents of the Indian Ocean, which has been our daily habit since we came to these shores. The beach is a very secluded one, and we had come to expect that we could enjoy our thalassic romps in the total confidence that not another living soul would be present to witness them. Imagine then our astonishment when, on emerging from the waters in a state of nature, we saw crawling towards us along the strand a poor bedraggled creature, near to death and stretching out an arm towards us in most piteous supplication.

Mrs Pittenden screamed and ran to fetch the servants; but I had seen the poor creature's piteous eyes, and I was not afraid. At first I did not know whether it was a man or a beast, and to tell the truth I did not care; never had I seen such sadness in a face, never such supplication, never had I known such confidence within my own heart that God had put me on that beach to relieve that creature's sadness. And he knew too; even then he knew that we have travelled far, for a meeting that would change the lives of both of us forever.

How my Albert – for that is what I call him, and is the name he loves to answer to – how Albert recovered his strength with my aid, how he became first my pet baboon, then – as he learnt apace – my servant, next my friend, and finally my lover and fiancé: all this must await a more leisured occasion, for I sometimes think that there are enough amusing, instructive and sentimental anecdotes relating to our meeting, our mutual instruction, and our strong and burgeoning love to fill a tidy volume which would well repay the perusal of many a curious young lady. For now, all that is needful for me to say is that I am the happiest girl in the world, and likely to be the happiest married woman.

*

True love is always strange, though, isn't it? Leonora, of course, is exceptional, even amongst those bold and unconventional travellers and wanderers of her time. She even looks exceptional – her face a perfect oval, her brow high and noble, a classic beauty except for her eyebrows, which meet in a single, dark, emphatic line above her nose, quite bushy, and rich with her unique spicy scent.

Albert loves her eyebrows. When they lie together he loves to trace their length with the pink tip of a long prehensile finger, or the pink tip of a long prehensile toe, or with the tip of his long pink tongue. He never thinks about his past life; he is content to have relinquished his status as a senior baboon. He knows he is not Leonora's toy. He does not yearn for Lpipi and the other females. Leonora is fearless and adventurous, and he is teaching her to make love while rocking in the branches of tall trees; she is showing a considerable aptitude. Last night, when they were lying peacefully together, his deep hairy chest to her smooth back, his long clever arms wound round and round her slender waist, her round warm bottom pressed into his lower belly sending its messages of love and healing, the tip of his soft hairy tail nestling gently in her ear, he touched the underside of her soft little toes with his hard hairy toes, and she curled her toes and held his with a strength not far short of the strength of a young female baboon. And she whispered to him that in an earlier life she too had been a monkey and known monkey life and made monkey love. And who is there to say that that was not the truth?

Credits

Some of these stories have appeared in other places or in other guises or both. 'Keeping It Clean', 'French Baby', and 'Working Well' all appeared in *Cosmopolitan*. 'Early Bird and Smiley Face' was first printed in *Encounter*, and also formed the basis of a BBC TV film entitled 'Ball-Trap on the Côte Sauvage'. 'Inappropriate Behaviour' started life as a seventy-five minute BBC TV film; the story printed here is the *cuisine minceur* version.

'Thanks Anyway' has a long and shoddy history: originally written as a TV film that never went into production, it was first recycled into a radio play called 'Campus Blues', complete with country music; the title song I recall had some lines that went:

>   Great Tradition
>   Fly fishin';
>   Teachin' an' research was m'only ambition
>   In the country of my dreams.

Now it has had open heart surgery and also sports a postmodernist ending which more or less reverses its original message. I dunno, maybe I should have left it layin' in the same position.

Some of the material in 'Into Europe' and 'Into Europe: two. Some Aspects of the Economy' was intended to form part of a film entitled 'Big Time in Bavaria', which may yet get made – though I doubt it.

And the rest are all brand new.

I am indebted to Steve Attridge, Bill Davies, and a short monograph by Professor Larmouth of the Salford University Information Technology Institute for some of the information about data viruses, Trojan horses, and the Moose.

And Bernadette Davis was kind enough to donate one of her dreams.

Also available in Minerva

Andrew Davies

GETTING HURT

'Brilliant' – *Sunday Correspondent*

'Davies writes honestly about sex, and knows the difference between desire and obsession. He scatters seeds of wisdom in the landscape of torn sensitivity' – *Sunday Times*

'A healthy lesson for anyone still old-fashioned enough to believe that it is only women's hearts that break and bleed' – *Guardian*

'A marvellous picture of a man whose obsessive love for a woman makes him disintegrate as a personality . . . The most compelling first novel I have read for some time' – *Bookseller*

'Andrew Davies's achievement is breathtaking' – *TLS*

In his own words, Charlie Cross is a bloke in love. A hard-drinking, chain-smoking lawyer, he is well-off, divorced and heading for trouble. When he meets Viola in an after-hours drinking club he knows instinctively that they could do each other harm. What follows is one man's record of a love affair, an erotic, savagely funny and heartfelt tale of destructive sexual passion.

Thomas Pynchon

VINELAND

Thomas Pynchon's first novel since *Gravity's Rainbow*.

'A major political novel about what America has been doing to itself, to its children, all these many years . . . One of America's great writers has, after long wanderings down his uncharted roads, come triumphantly home' – Salman Rushdie, *New York Times Book Review*

'Vintage stuff – funny, fantastically inventive, packed with improbable erudition' – *Times Literary Supplement*

'Exhilarating and wretchedly funny. The most important and mysterious writer of his generation' – *Time*

'*Vineland* is one of the funniest, most cleverly written, superbly characterized and beautifully structured books that I have read by a living author' – Michael Bracewell, *Time Out*

'An essential novel of our *fin de siècle*, a finger pointing the way out of the 1980s' – *USA Today*

'How this book towers . . . it is a political novel in the ambitious, exuberant, powerfully serious mode of *The Satanic Verses* . . . It is funny, very funny . . .' – Fay Weldon

'His descriptive powers are breathtaking . . . Pynchon proves once again to be the master of what might be called the highbrow conspiracy thriller' – *Wall Street Journal*

John Banville

THE BOOK OF EVIDENCE

'Freddie Montgomery is a gentleman first and a murderer
second . . . He has committed two crimes. He stole a
small Dutch master from a wealthy family friend, and he
murdered a chambermaid who caught him in the act. He
has little to say about the dead girl. He killed her,
he says, because he was physically capable of doing so.
She annoyed him. It made perfect sense to smash her
head in with a hammer. What he cannot understand, and
would desperately like to know, is why he was so moved
by an unattributed portrait of a plain middle-aged woman
that he felt compelled to steal it . . .

'I have read books that are as cleverly constructed as
this one and I can think of a few – not many – writers
who can match Banville's technical brilliance, but I have
read no other novel that illustrates so perfectly a single
epiphany. It is, in its cold, terrifying way, a masterpiece'
– Maureen Freely, *Literary Review*

'Compelling and brutally funny reading from a master of
his craft' – Patrick Gale, *Daily Telegraph*

'Banville must be fed up being told how beautifully he
writes, but on this occasion he has excelled himself in a
flawlessly flowing prose whose lyricism, patrician irony
and aching sense of loss are reminiscent of *Lolita*' –
Observer

'Completely compelling reading . . . not only entertains
but informs, startles and disturbs' – *Irish Independent*

Jenny Diski

NOTHING NATURAL

'*Nothing Natural* centres with illuminating precision on a sado-masochistic relationship. Rachel is in her thirties, a single parent admired by her friends for her self-sufficiency . . . But when she meets the compelling, sinister Joshua she discovers another side to herself . . . In a sense which horrifies her, she has found herself . . . An outstandingly well-written novel' – *New Statesman*

'Jenny Diski writes with an admirable lack of sensationalism about a difficult subject . . . an honest and startling look at the angry face of sex' – *Cosmopolitan*

Its efficiency and its loathsomeness are about equal' – Anthony Thwaite, *Observer*

'Absolutely terrifying' – Margaret Drabble

'Chillingly clever. Jenny Diski is a writer to follow' – Robert Nye, *Guardian*

'Galvanizing reading' – *Women's Review*

'Her combination of searching intelligence and remorseless, writerly precision is remarkable' – *The Listener*

'That rare beast, a sexual shocker written with integrity' – *London Magazine*

Susan Minot

LUST & OTHER STORIES

'For all the New York chic which surrounds them, the situations and dilemmas of Susan Minot's women could hardly be more classical. The women know they are going to lose and several of them try to guard themselves against attachment, to stay free, but their hearts are not in it. They know there is not much they can do about it, once a look, a touch, a night out changes everything. It's a bleak situation, but talking about it doesn't appear to help, and writing about it doesn't either, beyond a certain point, soon reached. The terseness of these laconic tales has its own telling decorum' – *London Review of Books*

'A sort of tenderness in the writing reminds me not a little of Raymond Carver at his best' – *Guardian*

'Susan Minot's prose is a rarity in this windy age. It is clean, shapely, with the directness and precision of a child's letter' – *Penelope Gilliatt*

'This collection of acrid little love-hate tales passes on the bad news about relationships in the barest, most unselfpitying of prose styles' – *The Times*

Robin Hemley

ALL YOU CAN EAT

Sharp, fast, moving and funny, the thirteen stories in this collection take a bracing, off-beat look under the surface of everyday life.

In this outstanding collection, Robin Hemley focuses with startling honesty and perceptiveness on the delusions and distractions we use to ward off pain: an orgy of syrupy sentiment at a pancake social that coats over the cracks in a marriage; bizarre funeral rites for a dead husband – a re-run of the first date; a desperate man digging a hole in his ex-wife's backyard; the ingenious cruelty of two boys who have lost their fathers; a lover in need of a breathing space out walking in the rain.

Impressive and highly entertaining, *All You Can Eat* marks the debut of a major new voice in contemporary fiction.

'Dazzling stories . . . filled with powerful surrealistic images' – *New York Times*

'Hemley is an urban writer of spark and vigour, with an alert and retentive eye for surfaces . . . sharp, facile, energized and *au fait*, Hemley will have a great deal to offer in future years' – *Times Literary Supplement*

'A balloon which soars on the giddy winds of imagination' – *Scotland on Sunday*

Rose Boyt

SEXUAL INTERCOURSE

A compelling and original first novel about family life.

'Boyt deploys her primal themes with remarkable
ingenuity and zest. Her pared-down prose style, which
alternates closely observed economical description of the
often disgusting details of food or bodies with dialogue of
genteel banality, produces a fine sense of menace
reminiscent of early Pinter or Orton' – *Observer*

'Boyt manipulates her cast of emotional retards with
skill and her menacing depiction of seedy suburbia is
reminiscent of McEwan at his murkiest' – *20/20*

'A grim but darkly humorous tale about the juxtaposition
of two one-parent families . . . Their off-centre dialogue
is acutely funny' – *Independent*

'A cycle of birth, marriage and death documented with a
curiously impressive and distasteful laconic relish.
Possibly Rose Boyt is about to become the George
Gissing of our day' – *London Review of Books*

'Her characters inhabit an eerie domestic landscape into
which the reader is steadily, effortlessly drawn' – *Irish
Independent*

Helen Simpson

FOUR BARE LEGS IN A BED

'Absolutely brilliant . . . the only book this year that's made me sick with envy' – Julie Burchill

'These stories of sex pack a truly original pungency . . . kicking off belly-laughs or melting you with an apt phrase, Simpson makes a delectable debut' – *Mail on Sunday*

'She can be sparingly tragic and unsparingly funny . . . a unique writer' – Ruth Rendell

'Outstanding . . . You should read her' – *The Times*

'Dazzlingly original . . . Simpson's black-hearted humour is something to relish' – *Sunday Times*

'Stories told in such succulent prose that you wince at their brevity . . . a most exceptional debut' – *Evening Standard*

'Deserves all the literary prizes she will get' – *Daily Telegraph*

Lynne Sharon Schwartz

LEAVING BROOKLYN

'This is the story of an eye and how it came into its own.'
Almost from birth, Audrey has had a wandering eye
which distorts the shapes of the actual world. Growing
up in the sheltered, provincial atmosphere of post-war
Brooklyn, she uses her double vision to create – and
recreate – her own reality. But social and family
pressures for conformity and perfection lead her to an
encounter which opens the path to an individual, adult
perspective.

'I read the book in one sitting, and it has stayed with me
for weeks now. This is Lynne Sharon Schwartz's best-
written book and, to me, her most moving. The blend of
lyricism and history, of memory and the imagination –
all shot through with the female erotic – is wonderful' –
Russell Banks

'Bracing, wise, boldly inventive . . . Lynne Sharon
Schwartz understands the fearful, self-imposing
innocence of Brooklyn in the post-war years – and why a
young girl hungry for reality and knowledge, would have
to leave it' – Joyce Johnson

'Stunning . . . so much deftness and brio. Coming of age,
one of the oldest of the ever-renewable, is seldom
registered as disarmingly as it is in *Leaving Brooklyn*' –
New York Times Book Review

Roddy Doyle

THE SNAPPER

'A superb creation, exploding with cheerful chauvinism and black Celtic humour. The dialogue crackles with wit and authenticity. The characterisation is superbly accomplished. Even the family dog rings true. You finish the book hungry for more and in no doubt that this is the real McCoy' – John Nicholson, *The Times*

'While recognising that we have all sat po-faced through novels which other people have assured us were hilarious . . . all I can say is that *The Snapper* creased me up' – Jonathan Coe, *Guardian*

'Not since I first delved into Flynn O'Brien have I so consistently laughed out loud while reading a book' – Peter Sheridan, *Sunday Tribune*

'Roddy Doyle's ear for low-life speech seems faultless: one feels trapped in a bus shelter full of Irishmen shouting obscenities and shrieking with laughter at their wit . . . Out of it come warmheartedness, and even tenderness, and a sense of the absurd incompatibilities of family life' – Isabel Quigly, *Financial Times*

'The most amazing account of a pregnancy ever written . . . absolutely perfect' – Maeve Binchy, *Irish Times*

THE MINERVA BOOK OF SHORT STORIES 3

Edited by Giles Gordon and David Hughes

The third *Minerva Book of Short Stories* continues the tradition of its highly successful predecessors. Taken from William Heinemann's *Best Short Stories 1990*, it contains excitingly varied work by twenty-five writers, some new, some established. Multi-faceted and diverse, vigorous and unpredictable, these stories range from the comic to the profoundly moving, the extravagantly inventive to the minutely etched. As the short story enjoys a deserved renaissance, this anthology confirms that it is alive and well and in good hands.

'An extremely bright gathering' – *Independent*

'A highly-regarded and highly-rewarding series . . . excellent and varied' – *Oxford Times*

'The level of quality in this collection is reassuringly high' – Anthony Quinton, *The Times*

Cecil Bonstein	Hanif Kureishi
William Boyd	Moy McCrory
Jenny Diski	Steve McGiffen
Janice Galloway	Adam Mars-Jones
Jane Gardam	Alice Munro
Nadine Gordimer	Philip Oakes
Robert Grossmith	David Park
Russell Hoban	Fiona Farrell Poole
Desmond Hogan	Frederic Raphael
Janette Turner Hospital	D. J. Taylor
Elizabeth Jolley	Jonathan Treitel
Gabriel Josipovici	Charles Wilkinson
Francis King	

Noel Coward

THE SHORT STORIES

This one-volume edition contains the complete
collection of Coward's short stories, twenty in all,
spanning fifty years of his working life. From shipboard
gossip at the Captain's table to backstage intrigues in
flower-filled dressing-rooms, from poolside champagne
breakfasts in Hollywood to suburban romances in
rooming-houses, the 'Master' reveals himself as a
consummate prose stylist, demonstrating why, for all his
success in virtually every other field of entertainment, he
returned again and again to the short story. 'I found them
fascinating to write,' he explained, 'but far from easy.'

'Coward is at his best when he is deflating the mannered
snobbery of the sort of people he must have lived with.
The descriptions of manners (or lack of them), the
understatement and the gentlemanly tone of the stories
provide few shocks and few laughs, rather a gentle
satisfaction at the end of each story. A wonderful bedside
companion' – *City Limits*

A Selected List of Titles Available from Minerva

While every effort is made to keep prices low, it is sometimes necessary to increase prices at short notice. Mandarin Paperbacks reserves the right to show new retail prices on covers which may differ from those previously advertised in the text or elsewhere.

The prices shown below were correct at the time of going to press.

Fiction

☐	7493 9026 3	**I Pass Like Night**	Jonathan Ames	£3.99 BX
☐	7493 9006 9	**The Tidewater Tales**	John Bath	£4.99 BX
☐	7493 9004 2	**A Casual Brutality**	Neil Blessondath	£4.50 BX
☐	7493 9028 2	**Interior**	Justin Cartwright	£3.99 BC
☐	7493 9002 6	**No Telephone to Heaven**	Michelle Cliff	£3.99 BX
☐	7493 9028 X	**Not Not While the Giro**	James Kelman	£4.50 BX
☐	7493 9011 5	**Parable of the Blind**	Gert Hofmann	£3.99 BC
☐	7493 9010 7	**The Inventor**	Jakov Lind	£3.99 BC
☐	7493 9003 4	**Fall of the Imam**	Nawal El Saadewi	£3.99 BC

Non-Fiction

☐	7493 9012 3	**Days in the Life**	Jonathon Green	£4.99 BC
☐	7493 9019 0	**In Search of J D Salinger**	Ian Hamilton	£4.99 BX
☐	7493 9023 9	**Stealing from a Deep Place**	Brian Hall	£3.99 BX
☐	7493 9005 0	**The Orton Diaries**	John Lahr	£5.99 BC
☐	7493 9014 X	**Nora**	Brenda Maddox	£6.99 BC

All these books are available at your bookshop or newsagent, or can be ordered direct from the publisher. Just tick the titles you want and fill in the form below. Available in:
BX: British Commonwealth excluding Canada
BC: British Commonwealth including Canada

Mandarin Paperbacks, Cash Sales Department, PO Box 11, Falmouth, Cornwall TR10 9EN.

Please send cheque or postal order, no currency, for purchase price quoted and allow the following for postage and packing:

UK	80p for the first book, 20p for each additional book ordered to a maximum charge of £2.00.
BFPO	80p for the first book, 20p for each additional book.
Overseas including Eire	£1.50 for the first book, £1.00 for the second and 30p for each additional book thereafter.

NAME (Block letters) ....

ADDRESS ....

....

....